Griz

By
Eve Langlais

(Kodiak Point, #5)

Copyright & Disclaimer

Copyright © January 2015, Eve Langlais
Cover Art by Aubrey Rose © October 2014
Edited by Devin Govaere
Copy Edited by Amanda L. Pederick
Produced in Canada

Published by Eve Langlais
1606 Main Street, PO Box 151
Stittsville, Ontario, Canada, K2S1A3
http://www.EveLanglais.com

ISBN-13: 978-1505433180
ISBN-10: 1505433185

Prologue

A couple of years ago, before the troubles in Kodiak Point began and the boys had just come back from the war… Except for Travis, of course. Just finishing a program at their small local college, and still living at home, he never got to wear a uniform or taste real adventure—and never would, not so long as his mother and her wooden spoon had a say.

Rawr!

The unexpected and extremely vibrant roar in his head made Travis wobble on his feet, which sent people scurrying. He couldn't blame them. A guy his size falling over could lead to some squished body parts and possible broken bones. Something he well knew given it happened to him during his scrawnier years when trying out for football.

What he couldn't figure out was why his bear felt a need to vocalize at all. Sure Travis was injured, hence why he walked into the emergency room of their local clinic—his second home due to his accident-prone nature. But he'd gotten hurt worse in the past.

His bear rawred again, a happy grumble that was, this time, also joined by a hunger. Not a hunger of the belly—his ma kept him too well fed for that—but of the body, as in his manparts waking up.

Hello, why the hell was he having a boner moment? He'd thought those days of uncontrollable urges done and an embarrassment he'd outgrown.

The reason for his arousal soon became clear.

Whilst his bear might have smelled her first, as soon as Travis got within a few feet of the reception desk he saw *her,* did a double take, and ogled.

There she stood. The woman of his dreams.

A perfect creature who made his heart race, his palms sweat, and his bear roar. It also rolled around in his head as if drunk on honey and berries, but he ignored the less-than-dignified response of his beast side because the woman of his dreams probably would frown at such an immature reaction.

See, the female he vowed in that moment to make his mate was a doctor. A hot, redheaded one. A woman older than him, he judged, but only by a few years. It added an extra layer in his instant lust for her.

A lust unrequited.

Given he was making those waiting in the reception area wince, what with his arm hanging at an awkward angle, a nurse quickly booked him in—no need to fill out forms when you were a regular—and had him perched on a bed.

It wasn't long before the redheaded goddess arrived at his bedside, where he sat holding his crooked arm courtesy of a football game that got a little rough. Also known as a future lecture from his mother about wearing equipment for sports.

As if a grizzly would stoop to wearing protective gear.

Only pussies—the cowardly kind, not the jungle cat variety—wore helmets and padding. And for those who might not know, calling any kind of feline a pussy never ended well, or without scars. Travis even bore a healthy respect for his mother's Siamese cats, especially since the night he woke with one perched on his chest, sucking the life from him. He let out a very undignified scream and his mother, arriving in hair curlers and brandishing a lamp, chided him, "Stop your ruckus. My baby kitty is just showing how much he likes you."

Showing affection indeed. He made sure to check his room now before going to bed, lest his mother's satanic pets try and steal his soul.

"What happened?" his future mate asked as she placed her clipboard on the bed and gently palpated the injured area with latex-covered fingers.

It sent a thrill through him.

"I caught the perfect pass, but Boris tackled me, and I didn't land right. Then Kyle landed on top of Boris, and, well—"

"You got squashed and your arm cracked."

"Yeah. But I scored." He shot her a smile, which might have worked better if she'd meet his gaze. Even if just once.

However, she didn't. Dr. Weller, the new doctor for the clan—whom he'd heard about through the grapevine, headed by his mother—barely paid him any notice as she splinted his broken arm so it would heal straight.

At twenty-two, fit, and with a deadly smile that ensured his mother kept him supplied with heavy-duty condoms, Travis wasn't used to women ignoring him.

He tried conversation. "So, you're the new doctor, eh? I hear you just moved here. Where from?"

"Anchorage."

Still no eye contact. Even Travis had to wonder at her odd bedside manner. It was almost as if she intentionally wouldn't meet his gaze.

Maybe because she feels the sizzling connection too.

But in that case, why pretend it wasn't there? Was it some doctor/patient thing or something worse? Like was she dating?

Only one way to find out. "Hey, I know we just met and all, but are you free for dinner tonight?"

Without raising her eyes, she replied, but completely ignored his question. "Be sure to keep the cast on for at least three days. Otherwise, if you shift the bone while it's healing, we'll have to break and reset it."

He couldn't help but roll his eyes. "I know. This isn't the first time I've broken something."

"For such a *young* man," emphasis on the young, "you seem quite accident prone. You have one of the thickest files around."

"What can I say, I'm a *vigorous* fellow." And yeah, he did emphasis it and threw in a dimpled smile for devastating effect.

Still nothing!

"Maybe you should think of enlisting. I hear the military is a good channel for boys and their extra testosterone." This jab did result in her meeting his gaze, her brown eyes dancing with mirth, even if her expression remained serious.

The remark hit home. His lips drooped. "I've thought about it, actually. But my mother…" He trailed off. Need he really say more?

The whole town knew his mother. Betty-Sue, queen of the baked goods and wielder of the mighty spoon. Even the slightest mention of him going anywhere for more than a night sent her into a despondent fit.

Part of it was overprotective theatrics, he knew that, but the second part was fear. Travis had lost his dad, his mom's true love and mate, on a simple training exercise for the military. A fluke accident that, in one stroke, took someone they both loved from their lives.

She recovered by smothering Travis, and because he not only adored his mother but also worried about losing her too, he allowed it.

Then chafed at it in his teens.

Then growled at it when he graduated and got stuck in Kodiak Point at their tiny rinky-dink excuse of a college. Campus consisted of less than thirty kids. So much for the frat boy experience.

As he'd neared graduation, he'd hinted at perhaps enlisting.

The result?

"I can't believe you'd do this to me," she wailed. "It's not bad enough the military made me a widow, but now they're going to steal my baby boy too? I'll be"—and yes, her lip trembled and her eyes welled with giant tears—"all alone."

Deep down, he knew she'd played him, that she overdid the drama, and yet, a part of him recognized he could meet his father's fate. While he could accept that risk, he knew it would utterly destroy his mother.

She might seem strong to those who'd crossed the bad side of her spoon, but Travis knew better. Ma needed him.

However, Travis couldn't tell Dr. Weller—the hottest thing he'd met in Kodiak Point since the time Boris convinced him to try his three alarm chili—his reasons for not joining though. He'd learned enough from the men he admired, Boris, Brody, Reid, and the town flirt, Kyle, to know he'd lose any chance at ever becoming a part of their manclub if he admitted to such a weakness.

His attempts at more idle chitchat with the doctor failed. Arm set in a cast with instructions to take it easy for a few days, she sent him on his way.

But he went back, kind of regularly as a matter of fact. Funny how he couldn't go a few weeks, sometimes days, without busting something. Of course, it wasn't exactly clumsiness but more his mouthiness that got him in trouble.

However, no matter how often he ran into Doctor Weller, the woman he was obsessed with but who wouldn't give him the time of day, he never received the slightest encouragement. On the contrary, after a while, it was almost as if she actively avoided him, leaving him to the less-than-tender care of her nursing staff, who didn't make his bear rumble in excitement or his heart pitter-patter.

Travis knew he should give up on Dr. Jess, especially once he found out she was already married to a military fellow serving overseas, but instead, the longer her hubby stayed away, the more he was convinced he and Jess were meant to be together.

He just didn't tell his mother. She would have beaten him with her spoon for sure if for one moment she suspected her baby boy was pining to leave her for another woman.

His shrink bought her new car on his sessions alone.

Chapter One

Present time in a garage with the door open, the smell of barbecue in the air, and already a few cases of beer ingested.

"I say we go after snake dude." And no, the suggestion wasn't alcohol-based.

Kyle was speaking of the bad guy who'd been plaguing the clan at Kodiak Point. It seemed a Naga was behind the attacks on the people living here, and when his latest attempt to screw with them failed, the sly snake slithered off for warmer parts.

But he left behind a crew of pissed-off shifters. Shifters whose testosterone demanded vengeance.

Except for Jess. As the clan's main doctor, she provided a sane voice of reason when the boys got together to plan. Not exactly an easy feat. Jess—short for Dr. Jessica Weller—often wondered if her predecessor didn't dump this task on her on purpose because, really, these guys weren't interested in minimizing danger to themselves. As far as she could tell, they were determined to single-handedly keep the factories who made bandages and splints in the black.

"I agree. Let's go whoop his ass—"

"Don't you mean tail?"

"—and skin him alive. I've always wanted a pair of snakeskin boots." Boris slapped a fist into his open palm. Someone was riled. The usually grunt-once-for-yes, two-for-no Boris didn't hide his excitement with his plan to chase down the enemy.

Reid, the alpha of Kodiak Point, and usually a cool-headed kind of guy, wasn't helping. "He doesn't have much of a head start. If we leave now, we could possibly still sniff out his trail and go after him."

"It's time we ended that prick, once and for all," Gene agreed.

"I'm in!" Brody announced. As if there was any doubt. The beta of their clan lived for any kind of excitement. And if that chance involved possible violence or injury, then count him in twice.

Brody possessed a file almost as thick as someone else she knew. Someone also at this meeting, a man she tried to ignore.

Fail.

As if she could ever ignore him. As soon as he entered a room, all her senses woke.

But she did her best to pretend he wasn't there. However, it was hard given someone had duct-taped the bear to a chair and then gagged him. Brody, she'd wager, with the help of Gene.

A few years younger than all of them, Travis—gorgeous as he was with those melting brown eyes and rakish blond hair, that she totally didn't notice—had an awful habit of talking. Talking without a filter to men who felt the best lesson was one served with a fist. A cuff. A wrestle. Make that anything physical.

Before anyone came to the erroneous conclusion that Travis was their poor, abused whipping boy, it should be noted he did it on purpose. He didn't know how to keep his paw out of his mouth, and he took each jab and black eye in stride, and with a grin.

A grin he didn't sport right now, given the gag and tape, but his bright eyes certainly followed the proceedings with interest.

"I'll have us booked on the next flight out. Actually, even better, I'll talk to my buddy with a plane and see if I can't finagle us a private charter. We'll pack our things tonight and head out in the morning for the city and the airport."

Fist bumps all around. Booyahs abounded. Testosterone levels rose.

Until Jess cleared her throat.

Utter silence fell. Impressive really given the crowd, then again, they'd learned over the past few years to pay attention when she spoke. She taught them that she wouldn't brook any nonsense, not as a doctor, not as a female, and not as a member of the clan council.

Only thirty and a woman in a mostly male dominated society didn't mean Jess kowtowed to any misplaced chauvinism—or stupidity. She stood her ground, and she spoke her piece. So when she became the focus of so many male gazes, she didn't squirm. They'd all come in to her office at one point with something that needed splinting, stitching, or jabbing with a needle. They knew better than to think they could intimidate her. And if they didn't heed her orders to rest, she shot their ass full of tranquilizers and enforced her orders.

The last time she did that to Boris, Jan, his mate, brought over the yummiest muffins—not that she admitted their scrumptiousness to anyone. Travis' mother would have started a baking war again, which on the surface sounded harmless, but since everyone was afraid to turn down her food, it led to an influx of folks with tummy aches from overeating and a flurry of dieting requests.

"First off, I will go on the record to say this is probably one of your most half-baked plans yet."

Gene rumbled. "Yet? I don't know. I can think of a few that started off worse and drunker."

"No kidding," Brody said with a chuckle. "The pink bunny on my ass is a daily reminder."

Reid, their alpha, rolled a big shoulder. "I'll admit it's kind of a piecemeal plan, but it's a long flight. We should have something better by the time we land."

"Or you'll wing it," Jess added. "Whatever. That's

not my real concern. It might surprise you to know that I don't disagree that you should go after this Naga creature and take care of him." To those who were shocked that she, a doctor who'd sworn to save lives, condoned the assassination of a person, keep in mind she'd spent the last year or so patching the results of the mini war waged by this unknown enemy.

And besides, her inner hawk wasn't squeamish when it came to the kill. In a world inhabited by predator and prey, ruthlessness was required to stay alive.

Mess with me, and I'll kill you. Of course, she'd never actually killed a person before, but she liked to think she could if she had to.

"So if you agree we should go, then what's the problem?" Gene asked.

Did they really need her to point out the obvious? Judging by their puzzled miens, they did. "The problem is all of you can't go."

At that declaration, their excitement dissipated, much like hot air balloons deflating.

Only Brody ventured to ask, "Why not?"

"First off, Reid, you have to stay here. Not only are you the leader of this clan, and needed in case this Naga escape is but a feint, but Tammy is due to have the babies anytime now." Given Reid's wife bore twins, and was already well into her third trimester, those cubs could come anytime. This wasn't something Reid should miss.

The rumble from Reid wasn't meant as a threat, more as recognition of her logic. At least Reid was one alpha who could take advice and criticism without killing the bearer of the news.

"Fine. I'll stay, but I don't see why the rest shouldn't go. Given what they're facing, I'd rather send whoever we can to take this prick down."

An unexpected vote in her attempt to keep their planning in check came from the least expected person,

Gene. "The doc has a point. You can't empty the town. For all we know, this is a smokescreen to draw us out. Send the best guys on a snake hunt, leaving the town almost undefended. I'm going to suggest only a handful of us go."

Brody rubbed his chin as he weighed in. "Actually, a handful might work better. I was talking earlier today to our old sarge. He's the one who confirmed the target landed in their area. He did also say if we ever popped over for a visit, or went on a hunt, to let him know. We're not the only ones interested in the snake. Seems our old unit has been having problems too."

A thoughtful expression appeared on Boris' face. "So it looks like we'd have possible reinforcements and access to equipment. Excellent. The airlines can be such assholes about letting me bring my guns on the plane." Boris never left home less than armed to the teeth. According to his wife, Jan—also a gun nut—there was nothing sexier than watching him strip all the various weapons from his body.

Personally, Jess couldn't picture the giant moose of a man doing any kind of striptease, but a certain handsome grizzly though…

She dug her nails into her palm to keep her mind focused.

As talk splintered off with Gene and Boris discussing the merits of the latest assault rifle, Kyle added his two cents. "In case we run into trouble, I think it best if I put tracking devices on everyone who's going. You know, just in case shit happens and we get captured again, or lost. Those sandstorms, as I recall, were deadly." Kyle, their resident technical expert, was all about gadgets. When it came to computers, while not an expert hacker, he had connections and skills that would prove useful. At home.

Jess cleared her throat again and ignored the ensuing groans. "While I think sending in a handpicked group is a great idea, given Kyle's computers and network are all centered here and there's no guarantee he could quickly set up a command center once you get there, he'd probably serve you better by staying put."

"What? No mission for me?" The caribou slapped his chest and mimed a faint. "You're killing me, doc."

With a wicked grin, Boris slapped Kyle none too gently on the back. "Don't worry, bud. I'll make sure to show our enemy what a man with a real rack looks like."

"Don't you dare compare those dull horns to my deadly set of antlers."

"Deadly?" Boris snorted. "I'll show you deadly." The two men stood toe to toe, their friendly rivalry a long-standing one.

"Enough. We don't have time right now to debate the racks." Reid stepped between them and prevented any fist throwing. For now. They'd probably tussle on their way out once the meeting was over.

"Yeah, what the boss said," Brody chimed in. "Besides, everyone knows it's all about the fangs and fur."

As voices rose in protest, Jess rolled her eyes and let out a whistle—a strident one.

With a wince, the boys—and, yes, despite their age and experience, they were no better at times than teenagers—shut up.

"Thanks, Doc." Reid acknowledged her before addressing the remaining group with a frown. "That leaves only Boris, Gene, and Brody. Not much of a hit squad."

"I think we should bring Layla," Brody suggested.

"Bring a girl?" Gene grimaced. Given his mate, Vicky, was not only human but sometimes prone to fainting, Jess could understand his concern. But in this case it was misplaced. Layla wasn't a shrinking violet.

Brody argued his reasoning. "Not just any girl. You know Layla's got powers we might find handy out there."

Did she ever have cool powers. While the inhabitants of Kodiak Point, for the most part, owned a beast, or avian, side, Layla was more exotic in nature. Some whispered magical.

She held the power to control animals and some insects. Not shapeshifters or humans thank goodness, but anything else with a weak mind was fair game.

Given her freaky ability, Jess could totally see the advantage Layla would bring to the group.

"What about Jan and her dad?" Reid mused aloud. "She's an awesome shot, and he's just plain nuts."

"Negative." Boris shook his head. "Neither of them is going anywhere. Jan's pregnant." He announced it starkly.

Boris might seem calm about it now, but he hadn't been a few days ago. More panicked than she'd ever seen him, Boris had rushed Jan into the emergency because he'd caught her puking and refusing to eat. It took only a quick test to confirm Jan's suspicions that she was breeding.

Poor Boris. The news shocked the man to the core, and Jess had to give him a few stitches after he hit the floor.

At the announcement in the garage, there was much backslapping and handshaking.

Once the excitement died down, Reid brought them back to their previous discussion. "Okay, so Jan's out, as is her dad so he can protect her while Boris is gone. That doesn't leave us with many choices."

No one paid the chair hopping up and down in the corner any mind.

Jess kept her gaze averted too. While not officially

15

on the council, the nosy grizzly was always underfoot. In her line of sight. Showing up driving everyone—most especially her—nuts. Although her nuts was of a different sort than the guys.

Given they couldn't keep Travis out, and he couldn't stop himself from talking and getting into trouble, they duct taped him to a seat and tucked him in the corner. A corner where he could watch and see everything going on.

Judging by his antics, he wanted to go on this crazy mission. The guys would probably have let him, too, if they weren't all so terrified of his mum.

Aunt Betty-Sue, the name she expected them all to call her, would never let her baby boy go off to a mini war. Not without starting one.

Funny how the guys weren't afraid to beat on Travis in the name of toughening the bear up, but no one dared do anything that would put them in a direct warpath with his mother. Taking Travis on a possibly deadly mission? Yeah, none of them would volunteer him for that.

After they bandied about a few more names that could go, vetoed them all for some reason or another, their core group remained Boris, Brody, Layla, and Gene.

And…Jess. "I'm going too."

For the umpteenth time that night, all eyes swung her way.

"You're what?" Reid asked.

"Given you're all idiots with no sense of how to take care of yourself, it might be a good idea if I tagged along. You know, to provide medical aid. I can also give you some eyes in the sky."

"But you don't have combat experience," Gene pointed out.

"No, but I do know how to fire a weapon, subdue a crazed shifter, and I don't faint at the sight of blood. I am also utterly tone deaf."

"What's that got to do with the mission?"

"While it's never been tested, it's been hypothesized in shifter medical circles that a Naga's voice is less likely to influence those who are strong-minded and tone deaf." She shrugged. "It could come in handy."

"But who will handle any medical problems while you're gone?"

"Dr. Carter is more than capable still. He often helps out if I get a heavy load." Retirement had proved less exciting than he'd hoped, and he tended to hang around the center quite a bit. He'd probably jump at the chance to come back full time for a bit.

To her surprise, they bought her reasons for going, or at least didn't argue. Did they suspect her true desire for joining this mission, namely to hunt down the husband who refused to come home? More than that, she hadn't heard from him in what, six months, maybe a bit longer, and it wasn't because he was missing in action or on a secret mission that didn't allow communication. Her dear hubby just wasn't talking to her.

Not talking.

Not visiting.

Not doing a gosh-darned husbandly thing.

And Jess was mighty tired of it.

Crash.

The loud noise came from the corner of the garage. Before she could register what happened, Travis hopped to his feet, tattered duct tape at his wrists and ankles, gag missing to shout, "I'm going too!"

The guys all eyed each other then the grinning grizzly.

As one, they all laughed, Jess included. As if Betty-Sue would ever let him go.

Chapter Two

"Over my dead body." His mother's exact words.

Travis' reply. "I have rope in the shed, and I'm not afraid to use it."

Because, really, he wouldn't kill his mother, but neither would he let her stand in his way of partaking in the mission.

As soon as Travis heard Jess volunteering to go, it became imperative he become a part of the group.

Nothing, not even the skull-patterned duct tape that strapped him to a chair would stand in his way. As if he'd let his lady—who wasn't quite his lady given she was married and not interested—go into danger without a mighty grizzly to watch her back.

With determination as his strength, he snapped his duct-tape prison to announce his intent to join them.

The laughter by the boys, while understood, was uncalled for. Sure, his mother wouldn't like it, but in the last few months, what with everything that happened to his clan, Travis had come to a few realizations.

One. Danger was everywhere. Even a usually quiet town like Kodiak Point could become a hotspot for nefarious activities. The snake dude who wanted to cause trouble didn't care that the folks here just wanted to live in peace. Travis wanted to be one of the guys who helped take him down. And his curious bear wondered if it was true—*does snake taste just like chicken?*

Two. His mother was perfectly capable of taking care of herself. Travis finally took the blinders from his eyes and faced the fact that the people of his clan, and that included the men, deferred to her. Actually, most were kind of scared of his ma. Despite her claims she needed Travis to protect her, he knew she would be fine on her own.

He could leave for a few weeks, and she'd survive. She might bankrupt their savings baking like a madwoman on a mission to feed the town to keep herself occupied, but at least everyone would have a nice layer of fat for the long winter.

Could Travis get hurt, or worse, if he went on this mission? Yes. But he could also die from a stray bullet or if his truck went through the ice when he did the long hauls in the winter over the treacherous ice plains.

He practiced these arguments in his head during the ride home from the meeting. Of course, when he did finally announce his plans—"Hey, Ma, I'm going with the boys to the desert to cut the head off the snake!"—the fine-tuned speeches devolved into—

"No." His mother didn't even turn away from the sink where she rinsed some blueberries that would get added to the pie shell sitting on the counter along with some sugar.

"I'm going. They need me."

"I need you." She turned and pinned him with her stare. The famous stare. The one that made him squirm and want to agree to anything she said.

It took only a thought of Jess, poor Jess all alone an ocean away, maybe making up with her estranged a-hole of a husband for him to fight the Medusa gaze. "Well, you'll have to do without me for a little while. The town and the boys need me more."

She uttered a very unladylike snort. "Oh please. What kind of aid do you think you can give those boys? You have no experience."

"And why is that, Ma?" he said, not without a little bit of irritation. "I'll tell you why. Because you won't let me do anything."

"To keep you safe."

"I'm not safe. You're suffocating me."

At that, she burst into tears and sobbed about how she tried so hard, and it was all because she loved him. However, Travis was finally wise to her tricks.

"Not working, Ma. Not this time," he stated as he jogged up the stairs to the second floor and his room.

She switched tactics, resorting to anger instead. "Of all the ungrateful things. I did my best by you, and this is how you would repay me?"

He didn't even bother replying to her tirade, which led to phase three—implanting self-doubt.

"You don't have the right skills, baby boy. You'll just get in their way. This type of thing calls for men of experience, not young boys."

Experience came from acting, not sitting at home twiddling his thumbs to make his overprotective mother happy. "I'm not a little boy anymore, Ma. I'm twenty-five freaking years old. Old enough to make my own choices and do what's right. I'm going, and that's final."

Travis finished shoveling clothes in his duffel bag while ignoring his mother, who stood only a few feet away with her wooden spoon. It wasn't easy. Instinct screamed he not turn his back lest she tan his hide.

However, he was a man now, not a cub. And, as a man, it was time he cut the apron strings she insisted on binding him in, starting with this trip.

More like a mission. A real one. Overseas and everything!

"But who will keep you safe?" This time, he spotted the real fear in her. The fear he wouldn't come home. That he'd leave her all alone, like his dad had.

His voice softened. "It's all right to be scared, Ma. But you can't keep me in a safe bubble forever. You have to trust me. Trust the guys I'm going with. You know Brody, Boris, and Gene all have mad skills when it comes to this kind of thing."

Poor cousin Reid couldn't go, not with his list of responsibilities. Someone needed to keep Kodiak Point running. The joys of leadership, something Travis most definitely did not crave. He had his hands full enough trying to keep his mother from running his life.

"I'll miss you," she said, her expression woebegone.

He relented a little and hugged the woman who'd raised him. He loved his ma, even if she was violently overprotective and scared all his friends—actually, anybody who knew her.

"I'll miss you too, but it's time for you to let me go."

"Promise you'll come back."

"I promise." And he'd do his best to keep it. Travis had plans, and they didn't include a sandy grave far from home.

"And don't you go falling for any of those local girls."

Not likely. Travis already had an eye on a woman, the fantastic Doctor Jess. Sure, she barely seemed to notice he was alive, but he planned to change that on this trip.

Hold on tight because I intend to show you a grizzly kind of love. Grrr.

Right after he figured out how to get rid of her husband.

I wonder if she'd flip if I accidentally murdered him?

He knew the town wouldn't fault him for it.

While no one had the heart to come out and tell the doc, everyone knew Frederick was a no-good prick. It was no secret that he could have come home years ago, yet chose not to. The absent husband didn't even have the decency to hide his various infidelities.

It appalled Travis, and many in the clan, that Jess' husband so cockily betrayed his vows. Worse, Jess had to know about it. In a town this small, gossip spread like wildfire.

As to how everyone knew? Frederick, a prick no one ever met but heard about, was serving with some shifters under the command of Reid's old rhino sergeant. When it came to their kind, it was a small world, and while they could keep the secret of their existence from humans, juicy gossip such as that about a guy who was avoiding his wife and worse, stepping out on her made the rounds.

So given Frederick's blatant infidelity, why didn't she divorce him? It wasn't because she was weak. On the contrary, the doc was one of the toughest-minded women he knew. And he knew quite a few.

He'd asked Reid one night while drunker than Eli, the town lush.

"The fucker's cheating on her left and fucking right," Travis had slurred. *"She hasn't seen him in years. Yet she doesn't divorce his ass and move on to someone better."* Someone who would worship her. Like me.

Reid, only nursing his beer and thus still able to speak logically, gave him the reason. "It's because of what she is. She can't help it. Red-tailed hawks mate for life. As in, so long as dickhead breathes, she can't move on, no matter how much she wants to."

"So I should kill him," was Travis' brilliant drunken deduction.

"Fuck yes. And fuck no."

Drunk or not, Travis could make no sense of the answer. "Hunh?"

"Yes, Frederick needs to die, but you can't kill him. Well, technically you could, and she'd be a widow, and if you covered your tracks right, I wouldn't have to judge you or nothing. But she would judge you. For all we know, she loves the cheating son of a bitch. Or she feels honor-bound to him. Or she might just be a woman and get pissy that you decided to change the course of her life without asking."

Well, someone needed to help her change it. Travis was getting tired of waiting for Frederick to catch some venereal disease and die or to meet the wrong guy in an alley at night and have his corpse found the next morning bled dry.

Surely there was something he could do? And that something wasn't allowing Jess to confront the prick on her own.

What if they reunited and all was forgiven, or if Frederick took one look at her and realized he'd been an idiot?

Then I'll go grizzly on his ass.

Really, though, that was one option he really hoped didn't come to pass. Who knew a grizzly could howl mournfully? Travis grimaced.

Then again, given the jerk's actions, perhaps he had worse to fear. What if this Frederick dude was a cold and callous bastard who made her cry?

Then maybe I'd have justification to kill him.

As Travis clambered into his truck, he noted it was way too early, or late depending on how you looked at it, to begin his drive to the airstrip. Yet, at the same time, he couldn't stay in the house and listen to his mother harangue him all night.

It was bad enough that, as he sat behind the wheel of his vehicle, she hollered from the porch. "You get back here right this instant, Travis Eustace Montgomery Huntley Junior!"

Ooh, he was in trouble. She used all his names.

He didn't care. A light bulb went off in his head as he got an idea. He pulled away from the curb and cranked the music so he wouldn't hear his mother's last yodels.

Boris was quieter in his reaction to his presence on his doorstep.

Slam.

The door just missed his nose. Must have been a draft that shut it. No way would his mentor leave him out in the cold.

He heard muffled voices, and a moment later, the portal swung open again, held by the ever-perfectly-groomed Jan.

As a teenager, he'd kind of lusted after her, but that all changed once Jess came along, and once the snow fox hooked up with his best buddy, the man code applied. "No touching, no looking."

"Why are you here?" Boris asked, not looking at all pleased. Given he wore only trackpants, while Jan sported a robe, Travis could only assume he'd woken them. Or not, given the flush on Jan's cheeks.

"I thought we'd get an early start in the morning and carpool."

"Your mother blew a gasket?" the moose guessed.

"To put it mildly."

"Of course you can spend the night." With a pointed look at her husband, Jan ushered Travis to the couch and supplied him with a pillow and blanket. As for his hosts, they slipped out of the house, Jan giggling, while he pretended to rest.

As if he'd sleep.

How could he?

I'm finally going on an adventure. And by the looks of it, Jess was finally doing something about her relationship status. Hopefully flipping her relationship status to single so he could make his move.

Rawr!

Chapter Three

I don't know if I can do this.

It was one thing to volunteer to go but another to actually realize, thousands of feet above the ocean where they flew—and not using her own wings—that Jess was on her way.

While the rest of the gang from Kodiak Point reclined in their seats, catching some shuteye before they landed and embarked on their mission, she stressed.

In less than a day I'm going to confront my husband, the man who left to serve his country and never came back. Even when given a choice.

Was there anything more humiliating than for a woman to know that her mate would choose the discomforts of military life and risk his limbs than return, even if just for a visit, to spend time with his wife? The only thing more crushing was the pitying glances and the whispers she couldn't help but hear that Frederick wasn't spending his time overseas alone. On the contrary, from what she gleaned, dear Freddy was quite the busy boy.

At first she'd cried. A classic response to infidelity—*Why? What did I do? Why doesn't he love me?*

Then she tried ignoring—*Out of sight, out of mind. Do I really care what he does?*

But, now on the cusp of thirty, with her hormones screaming to get some relief, and not just the kind a battery-fueled toy could give her, she was angry. More than angry. She was royally pissed.

How dare he be a coward and hide from me? I am his wife. His mate. He made a choice to marry me before he went to war. The fact that he changed his mind is too bad.

As a red-tailed hawk, Jess didn't have a choice.

Instinct, genes, and tradition made it impossible for her to move on. She'd mated Frederick, for better or worse, and until he died, she was stuck with him. So either she had to convince him it was time to come home—*or kill him.*

Honestly, at this point, murdering his sorry ass was looking better all the time.

So we can find a new mate. A vigorous one. Her bird wasn't bothered by her callous deduction. It even had a replacement in mind.

Travis.

No. She would not let her mind stray that way—even if her dreams did so almost nightly. It seemed forced abstinence had warped her sense of fidelity and taste in men.

For some reason, perhaps because Travis made sure to visit the emergency room on a regular basis, Jess' avian side—*Not me, never me*—had taken a shine to the bear. A real shine. One she'd now fought for years, and which only grew worse with time.

Given her loneliness, Jess didn't know how much longer she could fight the cuddly grizzly's dimpled and suggestive smiles. Deny the ardent heat in his eyes. Keep herself from mauling his tight, muscled bod.

The insane urge to do bad things with Travis—*bad but oh so good*—was why she sat on this ridiculously long flight, heading to some arid, dangerous place on a hunt for a madman. While theirs wasn't a military-condoned operation, they would be popping by the base camp where her husband resided. Once there, she would confront Frederick and force him to fulfill his duties as her husband—whether either of them liked it or not.

"Worried about the mission?"

Even without a keen sense of smell, she would have known who dropped into the seat beside her. Sitting by the window, Jess kept her gaze on the clouds drifting below them, wishing she were the one soaring on the air currents. Free.

Instead, she was stuck in a coffin with metal wings. *Ack*. It made her hawk tuck her beak in shame.

"Not worried. Just relaxing my mind. We won't really have a real sense of the situation until we land and reconnoiter."

"Reconnoiter." Travis laughed. "What an awesome word. I know this is supposed to be a serious trip and all, but I have to say, I'm psyched I came along."

Funny, because Jess really wished Travis hadn't. His close presence made it so hard to think. But she couldn't exactly tell him to move because his nearness aroused her—and made her want to join the mile high club.

Instead, she sought to dislodge him using a dirty ploy. "Way I hear it, Betty-Sue isn't too happy her little boy took off."

Okay, that was really low.

It wiped the smile from Travis' face, but his rarely seen glower didn't make him less appealing. On the contrary, this hint of darkness was sexy.

Would he notice if she whacked her head off the seat in front of her a few times to punish her dirty mind?

"Ma's high-strung. She'll get over it. A man's got to do the right thing, especially if it's beneficial to others."

The pointed gaze he shot her made her think he spoke directly to her, and perhaps he did.

Travis, like everyone else, surely knew of her mate's cheating ways. Yet, despite his attraction, surely Travis wasn't implying he would act?

Her heart rate sped up.

She ordered it to slow down.

The situation with Frederick was hers to deal with. She couldn't allow Travis, or anyone else, to interfere. Because if anyone deserved to peck the jerk's eyes out it was Jess!

"The right thing?" She snorted. "You know, I hear people say that, but sometimes I have to wonder, who decides what the right thing is? How can you know if you're making the proper choices?" She'd thought she knew what she was doing when she married Freddie while in her last year of medical school just before he got drafted.

Despite her high GPA, it panned out to be the dumbest thing she'd ever done.

"Sometimes you have to just go with what your gut says." How intently he stared at her as he said it.

She couldn't hold his gaze, not without perhaps giving something away of her inner turmoil. Time to remind him of a crucial fact. Remind them both. "I'll be seeing my husband while we're in staying in the military camp."

No denying the grimace at her words. "Yeah. I figured you would. Does he know you're coming?"

And give him a chance to disappear and rob her of her chance to confront him? "Nope. I thought I'd surprise him."

Concern filled his brown eyes, and he spoke softly. "Doc, are you sure that's a good idea? I mean, you haven't seen him—"

She cut him off. "I'm well aware of how long it's been since I've seen my husband. I don't think there's anyone who doesn't know. And, might I add, it's none of your business."

"It could be."

Now that wasn't subtle at all. It seemed the imminence of her reunion with Freddie made Travis bold. A part of her exulted in the fact that he wanted to care, but on the other hand, honor meant she had to reject his offer. Instead she avoided it. "I'm sorry. Would you mind moving so I can use the washroom?"

Had she chickened out of answering?

Yes. Yes, she had because she really feared the wrong words would slip out of her mouth. Words like, "Please make me your business. Oh, and would you take off your shirt? I'd like to examine you—with my tongue."

Chapter Four

Well, at least she hadn't said no.

But she sure escaped damned quick.

Travis allowed himself to stare at Jess' ass, which given the observant guys he traveled with, wasn't the brightest idea.

"Travis, stop staring at the doc's butt and get your hairy carcass over here," Brody called.

Caught.

Travis couldn't help but make a face at Brody as he realized he was going to have to trade his seat beside a hot hawk for one beside a glaring wolf. He'd probably get a lecture too.

Sometimes being the youngest in a group sucked. Holding in a sigh, he levered himself from his current spot and dropped himself into the empty seat beside Brody.

"What's up, boss?"

"Stop bugging the doc."

"Who says I was bugging her?" Travis replied.

"Are you going to tell me you weren't making big bear eyes at her?"

The biggest he could manage, not that they seemed to work. "So what if I was?"

"She's married, dude."

"To a douchebag."

"Yup. A douchebag we're going to run into in less than eight hours. You need to cool it around the doc."

"I haven't done a thing." Not laid a single hand on her, even though he was tempted.

"Never said you did, however, dude will only need to take one look at your googly eyes and he'll know.

Then kill you."

"He can try."

"And he'd probably succeed. Frederick might be an asshole, but he's a trained one. A deadly one."

"What makes you think he'll care who's staring at Jess? The man hasn't been home in over three years. Three, dude!"

"Just because he's been ignoring her doesn't mean he wants anyone else poaching. Guys like Frederick are funny that way."

"Not funny to me." Not when he stood between Travis and Jess. Sure, she'd never given him any indication she returned his interest, not openly, but Travis knew she felt something. Call it a sixth sense. Gut instinct. Whatever. He could also smell her arousal whenever he got too close, like just now. If Jess were single, Travis knew he could—

The slap in the back of the head forestalled any interesting thoughts on what he could do to the red-haired doctor.

He glared at Boris, who took a seat across the aisle from him. "That was uncalled for."

The big moose smirked. "So do something about it."

"And have Jan threaten to make me into a rug for your living room floor again? No thanks."

The vixen was fiercely protective where Boris was concerned. Ironic really given Boris was a borderline psychopath who would prefer to shoot first and drag it home for dinner.

He also used his cold gaze when playing poker. The moose could bluff like no one's business and take all of Travis' money.

Asshole.

"Scared of a cute, defenseless woman, imagine that," Brody mocked.

Even Boris had to laugh at the definition of Jan as defenseless. The woman could outshoot just about everyone but her dad.

Yet Boris, ornery moose Boris, reveled in her skills. "My Jan." A happy grunt of two words said it all. Boris was in love, and he didn't care who knew. Mock him though, and he'd gladly rearrange your face. Travis knew from experience.

Still though, if the grumpiest moose with mental issues could settle down with a hot babe like Jan, then there was hope for the rest of them.

Hell, even free-spirited Brody recently got hitched.

"Where's Layla?" Travis inquired. Brody's mate, some kind of weird witchy woman with a power over bugs and animals, tended to freak a lot of people out.

Except for Travis. He found anyone who could get a salmon to swim to him in shallow waters so he could swipe it when he went grizzly awesome.

"Napping in the back. Which is what we should all be doing."

"I would be if you'd all shut up," Gene grumbled from across them where he lay splayed, his eyes shuttered. "Yapping like little girls. It's fucking annoying."

"Go back to sleep, big man. You could use the beauty rest. I might even recommend you sleep for a few weeks." Travis' baiting met with only the smallest of growls. Gene didn't rise to the taunt about his looks, not since he'd found a geeky human who'd mistaken him for a hero.

Gene, the killer ghost, a deadly polar bear, the most feared man in their gang, a hero?

And they say I suffered one too many concussions.

Someone needed to check the prescription on that girl's glasses because Gene was ugly, but cool, except when he was slapping Travis down on a training mat and telling him to try harder.

He tuned back in to the conversation going on in hushed tones.

"Reid got a hold of Sergeant Carson."

"I still can't believe that old bastard is still running the camp," Boris stated with a shake of his head. "Damn, he's got to be what, fifty, sixty? I thought for sure he'd have retired. Then again, I haven't seen or talked to the rhino since we got our discharge."

"Oh, he's still there and still just as ornery as ever. But helpful. He's sent a vehicle to meet us at the airstrip. Apparently the military is most interested in our target. Seems there were problems a little over a year ago that the townsfolk were attributing to a snake god."

"Less god, more like shapeshifter."

Nagas were serpentine-based shifters, rare, mostly because their kind were hunted pretty much to extinction because they were so dangerous. A Naga could walk as a man, shift into an actual giant snake, or, if strong enough, do a half shift where, below the waist, they bore the tail and rattle of a snake, their skin sported scales, and their spit turned into venom. But what made them truly deadly was their speech in this half form. Their sibilant words could hypnotize a person into doing their bidding. The weaker the mind, the stronger the hold.

It explained how a stranger managed to convince a bunch of weak-minded shifters to attack Kodiak Point. What it didn't explain was why?

What had they done to earn such enmity?

Brody was still talking. "Once we hit base camp, Sarge is going to set us up with some gear, rations, and a vehicle."

"The military doesn't mind loaning?" Travis asked.

"When interests align, the military is open to lots of things."

"Do they have a trail for us to follow?"

"Kind of. According to sarge, the Naga hijacked a car at the airport and drove it out into the badlands."

"So they followed it?"

"To a certain extent. A sandstorm obliterated the traces of its passage, and given they were running low on supplies, they turned back. But, before that happened, I'll give you one guess as to what direction it was headed."

Gene growled. "It's gone to ground in those mountains where they held us prisoner."

By 'us', Gene meant himself, Reid, Brody, Boris, Kyle, and several others, most of whom died, not all of them in the detention camp. Some just couldn't handle the real world once they escaped.

Whatever happened to them while they were held captive was never openly spoken of, but the result was clear. The men returned different.

Harder.

Damaged.

They each dealt with their incarceration in different ways, some better than others.

Travis frowned as he thought aloud. "I thought Brody killed the snake that was in charge of that prison camp."

The bristling tension in Brody's body was evident as he straightened in his seat. "I did. Chopped his fucking head off myself before setting fire to the place. No way he survived."

"Yet another snake has risen to take his place," Boris pointed out. "Did he have a son or other relative perhaps that is seeking vengeance?"

"It would explain a lot," Brody mused.

"Still going to kill him," Gene announced, not opening his eyes but obviously not sleeping as he added his two bullets to the conversation.

"If we know where he's going, then why hasn't

the military moved in on the place to clear it out?" Travis couldn't help but note the anomaly in their discussion.

"Because," Jess replied as she passed them to regain her seat, "those mountains are technically not in territory they are allowed to enter. They're right over the border. To invade them might involve some sticky red tape they want to avoid."

"Hence why they're willing to give us supplies," Brody said, picking up the discussion, "but will deny any knowledge of our activities if we're caught."

"Bullshit politics." Boris grunted his disgust, and heads nodded all around.

"I, for one, am glad they're leaving it to us," Gene announced, rousing his head long enough to bare a feral grin.

A grin Boris echoed. "I am totally going to kick your ass in kills."

"Ha, you're both going to bow to my mighty wolf skills," Brody boasted.

Feeling the bonding moment, Travis added his own claim. "I'm going to grizzly some rebel ass."

For once they didn't laugh in mockery.

After that, they tried to rest. Well, Travis at least tried, but he failed.

Excitement thrummed through him. With any luck, this mission would finally elevate him in the eyes of the men he admired, and Jess would finally maybe see him as more than just a clumsy bear.

But if he was counting on luck, then he was in for a nasty surprise because, as soon as they landed, the worse kind befell him in the form of the person they'd sent to meet him.

None other than Jess' absent husband.

Crap.

Chapter Five

Of all the bad luck.

When Jess hit the wall of heat upon exiting the plane, she foolishly thought it was the only shock she'd have to deal with. However, the stifling, unbreathable air was nothing compared to the one of seeing Frederick, dressed in green fatigues and leaning against a military Humvee, smoking a cigarette.

Filthy habit. Just another thing about him that only served to heighten her dislike, and she did dislike him.

She'd often wondered over the past few years if once she set eyes upon Frederick—a good-looking guy at six foot two, built like a linebacker, with blue eyes and black hair, a true raven breed—she'd feel the attraction that once made her think she loved him.

Looking upon his chiseled visage, with its shadow of a beard, and seeing the muscled arms bared by his short-sleeved shirt, it amazed her to note she felt nothing.

Okay, not exactly nothing. Rage. Irritation. An urge to slap him, yes. But no arousal or sudden urge to beg him to come back to her and give her babies.

Considering he was supposed to be her mate, it shocked her.

He's supposed to be my husband. The man who will father my children. But right now, all he seemed was a stranger, one she could have walked by and never given a second glance.

Jess knew the moment Frederick spotted her. Gone was the lanky slouch. His eyes narrowed, and his brow furrowed.

Not happy to see me? The imp in her capitalized on

it as she hit the tarmac and strode over to him. Only once she stood a few feet away did she let a bright, yet false smile, stretch her lips. "Hi, honey. You don't seem glad to see me."

"What are you doing here?" His tone matched his expression.

"Funny you should ask that because that's one of the questions I have for you. What are you still doing here?"

"My duty."

"Your duty?" She couldn't help a bitter laugh. "Your duty isn't just to the military. It's also to your wife. Since you decided not to come home and fulfill that role, I decided it was time to come find you. Aren't you happy to see me?" she asked even if she could see the answer in his gaze.

His cold gaze.

He doesn't want me here, and she didn't need his terse, "Get out of here, Jess," for confirmation.

While it didn't hurt that he so quickly rejected her, it did fuel her irritation. Especially when he uttered that and turned to walk away.

Don't you fucking dare walk away from me, you bastard.

Ignoring their audience, she strode after him, determined to not let Frederick escape, although he tried with his long-legged stride to get off the tarmac.

She caught up to him and grabbed him by the arm. "You will not run away from me, Freddie. Not anymore."

He tore himself from her grip and rounded on her, blue eyes blazing. "You shouldn't have come here. You don't belong here."

"What else did you expect me to do? It's been what, over three years since you came home. Three!"

"I had shit to do."

"Liar. You were given options to visit in between

tours. Tours I might add you volunteered for. You could have come for a visit at least. Or how about something even more simple like a phone call or even an email? Something. Anything." She couldn't help the way her voice rose as she hammered at him, her irritation simmering over. Long past the point of tears, his coldness toward her didn't allow her to feel any hurt.

"I'll admit I might have acted a little aloof."

She snorted. "A little? We're married, Freddie. Married as in me and you forever. A couple, except in this case it seems there's just me."

"This really isn't the place to have this discussion," he muttered, shooting a dark look behind her.

Jess could just imagine the avid gazes and ears trained their way.

"Funny, but in the last few years, there's never been a time or place to talk because someone's been a chicken."

"I'm not a fucking coward." He took a menacing step toward her, his gaze mean and ugly.

How did it come to this? How did the boy who used to love me in college turn into this jerk?

"If you're not a yellow-bellied canary, then stop avoiding me. Stop hiding from our marriage."

"But that's just it," he yelled. "I don't want to be married. How much more blatant can I be?"

She expected the verbal slap, but it still stung when it hit. She didn't let anything show. The tears she'd once cried over him were long dried. "Oh, I'd say your actions have spoken quite clearly on the subject. Yet, the fact remains, we're mated, for life."

"So then die."

Now that stole the breath from her. No matter she'd jokingly thought of killing him, she'd never meant it. However, the way Frederick said it, the venom in his words, the hate in his eyes… What had she done to earn such hatred?

He was the one who'd wronged her. How dare he try to make her feel guilty?

"I wouldn't give you the satisfaction. God knows I regret tying my future to yours, but what's done is done. And just so you know, once I'm done here, hunting down this Naga creature, like it or not, you're coming back to Kodiak Point, and you will stay there until you give me a child."

"And if I don't?"

"Oh, you're going to whether you like it or not."

"Gonna tie to me a bed and seduce me? How kinky," he said with a sneer.

She couldn't help a shudder at the thought of him touching her. Husband or not, she would never abase herself that way. "No. I have no intention of ever letting you back in my bed. I will, however, set you up with an appointment with a sperm bank and harvest your little soldiers. Once you've donated some viable specimens, you can leave and do whatever the hell you like, but at least I'll have something out of this poor excuse for a marriage." A piss-poor plan, but the only option she'd come up with if Freddy wasn't willing to try and make things work.

"I won't do it."

"Like I said," she replied over her shoulder as she walked away from him, back to the Humvee, "you won't have a choice. I'll knock your ass out, pump you full of Viagra, and hook you to a milking machine if I have to. But one way or another, *husband,* I will get something out of this farce of a marriage."

With that final threat, she stalked away, feeling his gaze burning between her shoulder blades, the hate almost palpable.

But she wouldn't allow it to weaken her. Couldn't

give in to the wobble in her knees or the tightness in her chest.

I did it. I took control of my future.

Problem was, the outlook appeared even bleaker than she expected.

And lonely.

Chapter Six

It didn't take a genius to see the reunion between Jess and her husband wasn't going well. Not well at all.

Whatever fear Travis had harbored of them seeing each and flying into each other's arms evaporated the instant they laid eyes on each other.

The acrimonious tension between them could have been cut with a knife.

Travis didn't even realize he was walking toward Jess and Frederick until Boris stopped him, a hand on his chest.

"Don't do it, cub."

Don't do what? Smash that smug prick's face off the pavement until he gave Jess the respect she deserved? Don't switch shapes so he could go grizzly on his ass? Maybe rip an arm off and beat him with it?

"He's an asshole," he stated.

"Yup. But he's her asshole, and by the looks of it, she'd got it under control."

Yeah, by all appearances, Jess told Frederick an earful, and judging by his glower, Frederick didn't like it. However, it was the narrowed evil expression that crossed his face as Jess walked away that Travis truly didn't like.

"I don't trust him."

"Even if your reason isn't sound, I'd have to agree. The boy is emitting some seriously bad vibes."

Boris stringing more than a few words together? Travis shot him a look. Frederick, the dark raven, must have really set off the big moose's danger radar.

"Why do I get the impression you know something I don't?"

"I know lots of things you don't. It's what makes me superior to you." Boris shot him a smug look.

As if Travis would let it slide by. "You might know secrets and have a rack big enough to hang a full load of laundry, but my penis is bigger."

It didn't rile the big guy as expected. On the contrary, Boris shook his head. "First off, boy, it's not length that counts, but thickness. Second, technique always trumps length, and third, if you haven't figured out it's all about the honey you can eat, then you ain't doing it right."

"I eat honey." Just not in a while.

Okay, so Travis' reputation as a ladies man was a tad exaggerated. Travis boasted a lot, but in truth, he'd not been with many women, especially not once he met Jess, and none in the past few years. It just seemed like cheating somehow.

He knew he loved the doc. *She's my woman.* And one day, when he could get over the little hump of a problem with her being married and all, he wanted to be able to tell her with a clear conscience that even when they'd not been together he'd stayed true.

Not that he'd admit that to Boris.

He'd mock him. Take away the man card the guys had only recently given him—and which Travis had laminated.

Predators didn't admit to feelings. Flirts didn't admit they went home Friday and Saturday nights from the bar alone.

And, it seemed, women could get away with pointing out the obvious.

"Hey, Jess, want me to sting your asshole hubby with a few scorpions?" Layla asked, her freaky purple gaze dancing with mirth. Her lips twisted into a smirk. "Maybe get one to crawl into his bed and prick a certain sensitive part?"

Travis wasn't the only one to cup his groin.

A laugh bubbled from Jess. "What and finally give him the size he's always longed for? Screw that. He's not worth the bother."

Well, at least the doc wasn't pining over him. Yet, Travis couldn't help but wonder if it was a front. Rejection, even if expected, in such a public way, had to hurt.

So when they grabbed their luggage and piled it in the back of the Humvee and the Jeep, which also rolled onto the tarmac to join them, Travis made sure to sidle close enough to Jess so he could whisper. "He's an asshole. Say the word and I'll kick his ass."

For once, she didn't pretend to not hear him. Her gaze actually met his. "Thanks. It's nice to know not all men are jerks."

Not exactly a declaration of love—or a demand to make her a widow—but at least she saw him and recognized Travis was different. In a good way.

As they piled into the two vehicles, Jess in the Jeep away from her estranged husband, taking a spot in a back seat with Gene, Travis opted for the Humvee, hoping to get a sense of the guy he considered competition.

Say it like it was, more like an impediment, one he still wasn't quite sure how to overcome.

At first glance, Frederick appeared physically impressive, but Travis wasn't a little guy. So when it came to muscles and size, they were on par. Coloring wise, they were polar opposites with Frederick boasting dark hair, blue eyes, and a deep tan from his time in the sun while Travis sported more of a light gold on his skin with golden highlighted hair—his ma's words, not his—brown eyes and a much nicer demeanor.

Or at least a less abrasive one.

Brody kept trying to get a conversation going with

the guy, only to get nowhere.

"How big is the camp nowadays?" Brody asked from the front seat.

"That's restricted information."

"Who's in charge?"

"I'm not at liberty to say."

"When's your posting expire?"

"None of your fucking business."

The terse answers didn't deter Brody, nor did he lose his genial smile, a smile Travis knew all too well. It was the one that looked pleasant on the outside but meant he was about to throw a punch—in this case a verbal one.

"Listen, asshole, I understand you've got some kind of issue about your relationship with Jess, but I'm going to tell you right now that you better get over it."

"My relationship with my *wife*," said with an unmistakable sneer, "is none of your fucking business."

"Now see, this is where I'd have to disagree," Brody replied, his tone still low and even. "The doc is a member of my clan, and as such, her protection and well-being are my business."

"You her boyfriend?"

"No, I'm happily mated. And if you're implying Jess has been stepping out, then I'm going to have to disabuse you of that notion. The doc has been nothing but true to her vows, unlike someone else."

"I made a mistake."

"In not being discreet about cheating?"

"No, by getting married in the first place."

"Regret doesn't give you the right to fuck her over."

If Travis weren't getting an evil glare from Boris to keep his mouth shut, he might have said something, or fist pumped. Brody wasn't letting the prick off the hook.

"Not my fault her kind doesn't believe in

divorce."

"Is that why you're staying out here? Hoping to make her a widow?" Brody never came right out and said it, but one could almost read his implied threat—*Hey, I can kill you if you'd like.*

Bless his mate, Layla, for not having a filter on her speech at all. "If the big bird wants to die, I could arrange something. I like Jess. She deserves better than you."

That finally rattled their driver. His jaw tightened. "You can't threaten me. I'll report you, and friends in the military or not, you won't get away with it."

Boris leaned forward and rested an arm across the back of the driver's seat. "Boy, I've gotten away with more killings than I can count. Don't dare me. And don't ever threaten us."

A tic along the side of Frederick's jaw showed him struggling with his temper. "What do you want from me?"

"A solution to the doc's dilemma."

Um, hello, Travis had a solution. She needed a new mate.

Problem was, despite their threats, everyone let her current husband live. Worse, they'd given him food for thought.

What if they scare him into trying to patch things up with Jess?

Rawr.

Such a sad sound from his bear.

Even though he didn't utter it aloud, Boris, his best ol' pal, must have sensed his unhappiness, as he nudged him and whispered a cryptic, "Don't worry."

But Travis did worry. He worried he was about to lose his hawk to an undeserving raven.

He had to do something. But what?

He knew what his ma would do, bake him in a

pie, but Travis didn't have a recipe. Nor did he know what Jess wanted yet.

And to him, that was most important of all.

Chapter Seven

Still simmering from her confrontation with Freddy, Jess was glad she had another option for a ride, even if it had no top and the dust at times made her blink away tears.

Since two of the base soldiers took the front seat, she and Gene were perched in the back row, the wind stealing sound as they whipped along the roads, the façade of buildings flashing by.

In this part of the world, a person couldn't ignore the exoticness. It didn't just come from the locale with the lack of green spaces, the arid air, or blinding heat of the sun. The buildings were so much different from the vinyl siding or wooden shingle or logs she was used to back home.

Out here, things were made of sand or rock, cemented together, often whitewashed to keep the abodes cooler from the blazing sun.

The people were different too, the women covered head to toe, with only dark eyes peeking through narrow slits. The men, on the other hand, sported a variety of garb, from westernized style, shorts, track pants, and T-shirts, to army fatigues and robes.

Given she'd not donned any headwear, Jess couldn't help the feeling she shone like a beacon with her wild red hair whipping in the wind, and her pale white skin an invitation to sunburn.

Good thing she'd slathered herself with SPF 50 before they landed. Freckles she could handle. Appearing lobsterish, not so much.

Once they hit the edge of town, they picked up speed. It gave them an advantage as they took the lead on the mostly empty road and thus did not have to inhale the dust of any vehicles in front of them.

In an effort to focus on something other than her confrontation with Freddie, she tried to take in the things around her.

Their military escort was a pair of young recruits, boys, still wet behind the ears and very much human, which surprised her. She'd assumed this military camp, which catered to shifters and acted as a special unit, wouldn't have regular humans among their ranks. It seemed she'd surmised wrong. It made her wonder how well it worked.

Keeping a secret like that in close confines had to be challenging. She'd have asked the polar bear beside her, but she didn't know him too well.

While she'd met her companion, Gene, before at the clinic briefly, she'd never spoken much with him, although she was well acquainted with his human mate, Vicky, a timid girl who turned fierce if she thought her polar bear was being disparaged.

So given their lack of acquaintance she was surprised when he leaned close to say, "You know, I could solve your problem and make it look like an accident."

"Why does everyone keep offering to make me a widow?" she muttered.

"Because we're not stupid."

"Or bothered by manners."

"I don't think you need me to tell you that your hubby is an asshole."

"I think everyone at this point is well aware of that."

"I think what we don't get is why you don't just divorce him. Actually, I should say, the women don't get it. Us guys think you should just slit his throat and toss him in to a deep, dark pit."

"Hawks mate for life."

"Why?"

She blinked at his question. "What do you mean why? It's just how it is."

"Says who? I mean, if you decide to throw the bum out on his ear, are you going to get hit by lightning?"

"No." Or so she assumed.

"Will you drop dead?"

"Not that I know of."

"Is there like some secret Red Hawk league that will send assassins after you?"

"No. Of course not."

"Oh."

"You sound disappointed."

"Well yeah. Nothing like a little deadly intrigue to keep a guy on his toes you know."

"Are you off your meds?"

Gene shot her a smile, which, given his scarred face and the amount of tooth, was less than reassuring. "I don't take pills, doc. Especially not ones a shrink recommends. I'm just naturally charming."

"Lucky Vicky."

"Fucking straight. But seriously, why can't you unmate the prick?"

"I don't know. Because of something in my DNA." She honestly couldn't answer it. Oddly enough, she'd never questioned it because it was just one of those things that was taken for granted. The sun came up every day. Eli got drunk and streaked down Main Street every Halloween bellowing he was the ghost of his granddad. And red-tailed hawks mated for life.

"DNA deciding who you stay with? That's the biggest load of crap I ever heard."

Exasperated at his questions, and even more with the fact that he made her question a lifetime of doctrine, she snapped, "Why do you care? You're already hooked up. Why do you give a damn?"

"One, anyone can see you're getting fucked over. Two, I didn't like your husband. He smells off. And three, Vicky told me to do something about it. I'd hate to disappoint her."

Where was a wall or a desk for her to bang her head against when she needed one? "Well, thank Vicky for me, but, for now, let's not kill Freddy." Because if anyone was going to peck his eyes out or shove him off a cliff, it was her.

Because then I can get on with my life.

With Travis.

No, not Travis. Let's try not jumping from one situation to another.

Why?

Why indeed. Because for one, he was about four or five years younger than her.

But given his antics he could use a firm hand to keep him in line. Besides, he doesn't seem to care about the tiny age gap.

Travis was misguided. Tempted by the forbidden. He just thought he wanted her because she kept rejecting him.

Which is why he's spent three years chasing me.

And not dating.

Travis had spent the last couple of years single. While she'd caught glimpses of him smiling, flirting—and driving her insane with jealousy—she'd never once actually seen him hook up with someone. And in a town their size, she'd know.

He's been truer to me than my own husband.

Husband. Ha.

Funny how she could use that term in regards to Freddy and not feel a damned thing. Nothing. He was a stranger to her.

Worse than a stranger, she didn't like him. Not one bit.

If, she, the girl who once knew and loved him, couldn't stand him, was it any wonder the people she traveled with wanted to kill him?

"Duck!"

Jess didn't have time to ask why as Gene shoved her head down. The crack of gunfire sounded only a second after.

"Someone's shooting at us?" she said, flabbergasted.

"Yup," was Gene's loquacious reply. Then again, why waste time explaining the obvious when he could slide his hand between the seats to snag the pistol of the soldier in the front?

"Hey," the young recruit exclaimed. His last words as it turned out because, a moment later, he slumped sideways, and the coppery scent of flood filled the rushing air.

"Hold on." The Jeep swerved as the driver did his best to make them less of a target.

"Excellent. Now we're talking a challenge," Gene enthused, aiming his gun at the rocky hillocks lining the road, a hundred or so yards out.

She wondered at his target until she saw the glint of sunlight off something metal.

Bang!

A moment later, their driver keeled forward, his face smashing onto the steering wheel and the horn.

The loud blaring, though, wasn't as worrisome as the fact that his foot still pressed on the gas, but with no active hands steering, they careened out of control.

"Shit," Gene cursed. "I'm going to unbuckle the driver and shove him out. Get ready to climb into his seat and drive."

"Are you fucking nuts? Wait, what am I asking? I saw the reports. You are," she muttered to herself in an attempt to calm her nerves.

"Now."

Gene no sooner hit the seat belt trigger than he was grabbing the limp body and tossing him out of the Jeep. The lack of pressure on the gas meant they began to slow, but not quick enough, and time was of essence, because, if she wasn't mistaken, straight ahead of them was a cliff.

Jess dove between the seats and scrambled to seat herself in the driver's spot.

In the back, she heard the *pop, pop, pop* as Gene fired at their assailant.

Pumping the brake, she attempted to slow their mad momentum while at the same time angling them away from the steep edge.

Neither action gave her the desired response.

The brake lowered to the floor without any pressure, and the steering wheel spun uselessly.

"What the fuck are you doing?" Gene shouted. "Stop the Jeep."

"I can't, they're not working," she yelled in reply. "Jump."

He did. Obeying without question, trusting her assessment.

How's it look, Doc?

Dire.

She would have followed Gene, except the vehicle hit a rock, and for a second, she was airborne, unnaturally and unexpectedly. Her head rapped the roll bar overhead and split the skin of her temple.

Warm blood gushed down part of her face, and she shook her head, dazed by the impact.

Not a severe injury, yet the incident cost her precious time. There was no time left. No chance for her to jump safely—if roadrashed and bruised—to the ground.

The Jeep shot off the cliff and, for a moment,

hung suspended in the air before it plummeted, her still in it.

Chapter Eight

The tension in the Humvee didn't lessen with the miles. Nor did conversation flow. A stagnant silence permeated the cabin, the fault of their driver who tight-fisted his steering wheel and glared out the windshield.

The brilliant idea Travis had gotten to ride with the raven now cloyed. The myriad scents bothered his bear, as did the close confines of the vehicle. His beast paced the confines of his mind, snuffling and anxious, projecting an aura of danger, which Travis surmised arose because of his own inherent dislike of their driver.

Determined to hate Frederick on principal, after meeting the jerk, he now just hated him plain and simple. Even were he not mated to Jess, the guy would have grated on his nerves. Just like he irritated Brody, who kept a wary eye on him, and Boris, who idly toyed with a knife—which he'd acquired from who knew where. As for Layla, she appeared at rest with her eyes closed, but somehow Travis doubted she slept. More than likely she attempted to communicate with some of the wildlife around them. Although how she managed that from a moving vehicle, he wouldn't hazard to guess.

The Jeep, with the other members of their merry band, had pulled ahead of the Humvee, far enough that Travis couldn't discern Jess's red hair, not through the plume of dust they left in their wake.

Yet, neither the cloud of particles nor their closed and almost soundproof cabin could mask the crack of someone shooting.

Spines instantly straightened, gazes turned to the nearest windows as they peered about, seeking the source.

Only their driver seemed unconcerned. His

trajectory never wavering.

"That's gunfire. Is someone aiming at us?" Brody asked, one hand braced on the dash as he craned forward straining to see.

"Negative," Boris replied. "The shots appear to be coming from up ahead."

It didn't take a genius to grasp the implication.

Someone is shooting at the Jeep. Jess!

"Fuck, and them without a cover. And I can't see a goddamned thing. Master Corporal, can you radio the Jeep and see if they're okay?" Brody asked Frederick.

"Try the walkie-talkie. It's in the console between the seats."

As Brody dug it out, Boris sheathed his knife.

"I need a gun," Boris stated.

The words Travis never thought to hear from the moose made Travis blurt out, "You're not armed? Since when do you not carry a gun?"

"Since you can't board a fucking aircraft with a bloody nail file."

"But you have a knife."

"A knife I borrowed when I used the men's room at the airstrip. Some local thought he could intimidate me. I taught him otherwise."

"How come we don't have guns?" Travis mused aloud. "I thought the military was supposed to be helping us."

"Because pinhead here didn't think to bring us any." Boris glared.

Frederick didn't even bother to give a glance as he replied, "I'm not authorized to—"

At his repeated standard answer, Brody growled. "Yeah, we get that, and I have to say it's mighty convenient, for the enemy I might add, that you're claiming that."

"Are you accusing me of being a traitor?"

"Nope. Just saying it's mighty suspicious that not only were we not armed as expected upon arrival, but now we're under attack."

Without a word, the corporal withdrew his sidearm—almost died as Boris lunged forward in reaction—and handed the gun to Boris.

The moose grasped it and leaned back, his deadly instinct restrained for the moment, but Travis could still sense the suspicion. "That's better, birdman. Maybe I won't pluck you for dinner today."

A shame. It would have solved a few problems.

"What about weapons for the rest of us?" Brody asked.

To his surprise, Frederick jerked a thumb at the rear. "We keep a few spare guns and ammo in the back."

"Travis, grab them, would you?"

Easier said than done. He humped himself over the top of the seat and dropped into the back with their luggage. Buried under their bags, he found a locked case.

Ha, as if that puny padlock could stop him. His bear had broken tougher things than that before in pursuit of a prank. Grasping the metal in a fist, he crushed it and popped it open. He flung the hunk of metal to the side and opened the metal coffer.

"It's empty."

Before they could process this unexpected setback, they came across a shocking scene.

They'd caught up to the Jeep, in a sense. The open-top vehicle careened wildly, off the road to their left. As Travis watched, he saw a body go flying from it and a distinctive redhead climb over the seats, dropping into the driver seat. Gene stood in the back, one arm looped around the oh shit bar while his free hand leveled a gun toward a hilly area rife with hiding spots.

The distinctive sound of more shots firing filled Travis with cold dread.

Layla uttered a gasp, and Travis gaped as Gene suddenly leapt from the moving vehicle, only to whisper under his breath, "No," as he noted the reason why.

A cliff loomed ahead. A cliff the Jeep couldn't avoid.

Off it flew. The vehicle hung suspended in the air, its wheels spinning uselessly, going nowhere but down.

With Jess still sitting in it.

Rawr!

Given the danger to Jess, he couldn't have controlled his bear if he tried.

He burst free from his skin, nails and hair sprouting with ridiculous speed, the pain of the shift masked by his fear-induced adrenaline. Problem was, large as the Humvee was, given the luggage and the tight area, it confined him.

Not for long. With a roar, he barreled out the back of the Humvee, the rear hatch no match for a determined grizzly.

On four paws, his claws gripping the hard-packed dirt and rocky surface, he tore toward the cliff's edge, passing Gene, who barked at him to take cover because bullets still hit the ground, their impact creating puffs of dust.

But Travis couldn't slow his mad dash.

Jess went over a cliff.

Jess. Went. Over. A. Fucking. Cliff!

The scene replayed itself over and over along with the word he wanted to deny but couldn't help repeating.

Dead. Dead. Dead. No one could survive a drop like that. No human body, not even a shifter, could withstand that kind of impact.

Unless that shifter had wings.

A pissed off *kree* sound rose from the chasm. Travis skidded to a halt, mere feet from the edge just as a massive bird flapped its wings and rose from the abyss.

Jess.

While he'd never before seen her in her bird shape—the avian species really restricted when it came to shifting because, while the other shifters in their animal shape could pass human detection, massive birds couldn't—-there was no denying the giant hawk before him with her glorious plumage of brown and white, which ended in a red tail, was Jess. It didn't take her strident shriek or the angry glint in her eye for him to perceive she was pissed.

Who could blame her? Travis wasn't exactly a friendly-feeling Yogi at the moment either.

With a screaming cry, she soared high in the sky, high enough he had to crane to see her.

The brilliant sun blinded him, and it must have blinded the gunman as well because, when Jess reappeared, rocketing from the sky as a silent missile, the idiot taking potshots at them never spotted her.

Then again, Travis might have helped with that given he was charging toward him roaring his intent.

Rawr – I'm going to tear into your soft flesh.

Rawr-rawr-rawr-ra-rawr. And then I'm going to tear off your head, shove it up your ass, stomp on you, and make you wish you'd called in sick today to your insurgent boss.

Yeah. That was an awesome grizzly plan.

Except his hawk beat him to their target.

With a caw of triumph, Jess plowed into the guy, clawed feet extended and knocked him from his perch.

With a scream, the fellow fell and landed with a crunch.

Dinner?

His bear, undaunted by the fact that they'd not gotten the kill, still wondered if they'd eat fresh. At home, he'd taught his bear to not kill wastefully, but apparently, he'd need to remind his furry side that they didn't eat humans.

Not human. Else.

Even before they reached the robed body, his nose detected the fact that the corpse was shifter-based. And of a kind he'd never smelled before.

As if hearing his unspoken query, Gene, who'd reached the body first, said, "He's a striped hyena. Real common for this part of the world. Dumber than shit too."

"He'd have to be to attack us," Brody replied as he arrived at a jog. "Was he alone?"

"Given furball over here has stopped roaring"— Gene inclined his head at Travis, who waved a paw— "and the fact Dr. Hawk, who likes to make an entrance, is perched pruning her tail feathers and probably thinking of how tasty your driver's eyeballs are, I'd say the area is clear."

"Only one guy? That's not much of an attack," Brody mused aloud.

"Less an attack and more a crime of opportunity, I'd wager. Hyenas are scavengers. Could be this one saw the lone Jeep and thought it would make an easy target."

Jess let out a caw at that, and Travis chuffed. Easy? With Gene aboard, the guy had signed his death warrant the moment he fired the first shot.

But it did make his blood run cold to think Jess could have been hurt. Maybe killed.

It bothered him even more when she fluttered to the Humvee and shifted shapes, grabbing the clothes Layla handed her and quickly donning them.

Travis and the others quickly averted their gaze, but it burned him to note Frederick, off to the side, leaned against a boulder and smoked a cigarette, not bothering to hide the fact that he stared with a brooding expression at Jess.

Jealousy burned within, hot and bright. He didn't even know he growled and that his fur bristled until Layla placed a hand on him and whispered, "Calm yourself, Travis. Like it or not, he's the only one with a legal right to stare."

He grumbled.

"I don't like it either, but until Jess gives us permission or does something herself, we have to accept it. Or at least wait until there's no witnesses."

If Travis could have laughed, he would have. As it was, knowing he wasn't alone in his contempt of the prick helped.

Once someone found him some clothes—because of course his duffel bag was in the Jeep that flew off the cliff—they were on their way, if a little crammed, in the Humvee, which could handle up to seven passengers but, given the size of the passengers, was cozy.

Yet Travis didn't mind because on purpose, or by chance, he got to share the backseat with Jess, and when he brazenly squeezed his fingers around hers, she left them in his grip.

Best day ever.

Chapter Nine

Worse day ever.

Crammed into a vehicle, her outward appearance calm but her inner nerves quaking, Jess really doubted the wisdom of her choice in coming here. Only a few hours on the ground and she'd gone through too much turmoil.

First, she had to contend with her ugly confrontation with Freddy, and then, someone had tried to kill her. Well, not just her, the whole crew riding in the Jeep, but still, at the moment, all she could truly focus on was how close she'd come to dying.

If not for Gene's excellent reflexes and the fact that she had wings, she'd have ended up dead. A splotch of red on jagged rocks thousands of miles from home.

And for what? Why? Because she foolishly thought confronting her husband would accomplish something. All it did was slap her in the face with the fact that her future stretched even bleaker and lonelier than expected.

The only bright light out of the day's wretchedness? There was one person who seemed to really care if she lived or died. And surprise, it wasn't her husband.

While Gene did his best to save her, the one who showed his true emotions was Travis. As the grizzly came barreling for the cliff, his roar and mad dash announced loudly and publicly how he felt toward her.

He cares about me. And he wasn't afraid to show it.

Although to be fair, while a little more vocal and blatant in his display, he wasn't alone. Actually, all of the men of Kodiak Point showed relief that she'd survived, slapping her on the back like one of the guys. Only Layla kept her hands to herself and said, "Nice escape. What number is it?"

Jess had blinked. "What do you mean number?"

"I used to number my escapes. Mind you, mine were escapes from prison, but in your case, I think we could say an escape from death counts. I think we should call it escape #1, the Cliffside Plunge."

"I think I'd rather skip any more escapes. I don't know if my bird heart can handle it." Indeed her pulse still raced from the adrenaline of the whole thing.

Yet, it stuttered even faster and more erratically when Travis took a seat beside her in the rearmost row of the Humvee and took her hand in his.

It warmed the cold spot inside her that couldn't help but recall the disappointment on Freddie's face when she'd soared over the precipice and landed, safe and unharmed.

Sorry, you won't become a widower today.

Having seen his expression, she wasn't too shocked when he muttered for her ears alone, "Almost, dear wife. Next time maybe I'll be luckier."

So much for a happy resolution to their situation and so much for her foolish plan to drag Freddie home as a sperm donor. Not because she couldn't nab him—she knew enough medleys of drugs to make him compliant— more that she didn't want him to be the father of her children.

Who wanted an asshole as a father?

She wouldn't subject her children to that.

But that still left her with a dilemma. She was married, mated, and yet holding the hand of another man while within spitting distance of her husband.

Maybe I do have a death wish.

The danger of her action didn't make her draw her fingers away.

The mood in the truck proved somber and quiet,

although the static from the radio did fill in the silent gaps. No one spoke of what happened, not because they didn't want to but because there was someone amongst them that didn't belong.

Oblivious to their suspicion or choosing to ignore it, Freddie drove the truck with a single-mindedness that brooked no conversation.

Given the recent narrow escape, everyone entered an intense zone of watchfulness. Brody surreptitiously kept an eye on Freddie. Head leaned back, Layla meditated, her hair floating and her eyes closed as she probably communed with the wildlife. Gene and Boris shared the spot beside her, squished side-by-side, attempting to give her some space. Given their grim profiles, they probably plotted death and maybe a little destruction. As for Travis...

He leaned over and whispered, "I didn't get to say this before, but your birdy has a nice tail." It wouldn't have sounded so wicked if he hadn't combined his remark with a mischievous wink.

She couldn't help the giggle, one that made her the sharp focus of their driver. In the rearview mirror, she noted his frown. Screw him.

"Your tail is a lot wider as a bear," she teased, for once not willing to push him away, not when his fingers clasped hers in a show of affection she needed right now.

"All muscle, doc."

Yes indeed, his human butt was at least. It wasn't just the doctor in her that could admire his perfect musculature, but the woman really thought his ass looked good in a pair of tight jeans.

I must be more rattled than I thought to be thinking of his butt at a time like this.

The rest of the ride to the base passed without incident. They hit a perimeter security check where armed guards perused their passports and checked all their identities against a checklist. A brief overview of their incident was relayed, and they had to allow a quick check of the surviving luggage before they were waved through.

Jess's first view of camp proved underwhelming. This wasn't *M*A*S*H*, or some kind of television reality show. The tents, set up in neat rows, were a brownish color that practically blended in with the ground. Each was pretty much identical in size and shape, the aisles between them uncluttered. Here and there she could spot men in combat fatigues moving about, all of them armed, some of them shifters like her.

How could she tell? Some used smell to differentiate human from her kind, but Jess, as a doctor, didn't need a scent to identify them. There was something in the way a shifter carried themselves, a certain gleam in their eye, and an invisible aura that she more sensed than saw that always let her know who she dealt with.

Given the size of the camp, she found herself surprised at the lack of soldiers milling around. Out training or in the field? She didn't know. This whole mission was new for her. And with everything that had happened so far, not something she was apt to ever repeat.

As they weaved their way among the canvas buildings, they didn't bump into any problems or questions. Freddie, whom they'd yet to ditch, led them to a tent and said, "Here's your quarters."

Without further explanation, or even a goodbye, he left.

Good riddance. A layer of tension she'd not realized gripped her, eased. With Frederick gone, she felt safer. How sad, yet true.

No one else seemed to care the raven left without giving them more instructions, although she did note that Travis wasn't the only one glaring at her husband's receding back. Boris kept a watchful eye too.

Brody led the way inside their temporary home. The large space was utilitarian in appearance. Eight cots, sheets folded and placed across the foot, eight small, battered chests for their belongings, and not much else.

The bags remaining to them hit the floor as they flopped onto mattresses. Fatigue, more the mental than body kind, overwhelmed her. Jess closed her eyes as she allowed emotional exhaustion to consume her for a moment.

A nap, however, wasn't in the cards.

"You made it." The statement was from a stranger, and Jess wasn't alone in suddenly coming to attention to greet the man who entered the tent with a stealth she found unnerving. However, it seemed he didn't take them all unaware. She noted Boris tucking a gun away, and Gene, alongside the tent entrance, discreetly sheathing a knife.

Good to know someone, or two, kept a watchful eye. As for Travis, no surprise, he'd placed himself between the cots, shielding her with his body.

Stupid bear. It really irritated her how kept doing stuff to show he cared. How was she supposed to remain aloof, to remind herself that not only was she—unhappily—married, but older than him to boot?

Or is it time I stopped giving myself reasons to push him away?

Something to ponder later perhaps when there wasn't a stranger in their midst.

She eyed the newcomer. A big fellow, he wasn't fat, but he was certainly wide. Given the wrinkled features, pure white hair cut in a short brush cut and weathered appearance overall, she put him in his late fifties or sixties. He was also dressed in uniform.

"Sarge!" Brody's face creased in a smile at the man's appearance. "I was wondering when I'd run into you."

"It's Master Sergeant now, soldier."

"Congratulations! I hadn't heard."

The old man cracked a smile. "The promotion just came down from high above a few days ago. I'm getting my new bars later this week."

"About time," Boris said, approaching to shake the man's hand once Brody released it.

"Perhaps, but the slow-moving cogs of the military are not why you've traveled a few thousand miles. According to the conversation I had with Brody and Reid, you're here chasing a certain pesky Naga."

"Pesky? More like pain in everyone's fucking ass. This particular serpent has been plaguing Kodiak Point for a while now. And wouldn't it figure when we finally managed to corner and confront it, the coward fled."

"Fled but didn't manage to completely wipe its tracks. You're in luck. The one you seek is out here," the rhino confirmed. "Even better, we have the go-head to apprehend him. We don't need another one of those serpent types slithering around. The last one caused way too much trouble."

"You think?" grumbled Gene. "I still can't see a mouse or a rat without taking out a gun to blow its head off." A reference to the time the polar bear spent imprisoned, and tortured. To say Gene still had issues was putting it mildly. Most of the men who'd spent time in the prison camp had returned damaged in some way.

"Oh come on, it wasn't that bad. At least the vermin provided some protein to go with our mush diet," Brody teased.

Boris shuddered. "Don't remind me. I still can't see porridge without breaking into a cold sweat. You wouldn't believe how long it took after that time in the insurgent prison before my rack regained its luster."

As a moose, Boris had one pride and joy—other than Jan, his wife—his antlers. Jess learned early on how sensitive he was about them.

Not that Travis ever seemed to care, or as he'd said after he ended up in the emergency room after a friendly scuffle with Boris, "But, Doc, it wasn't really my fault. I simply asked him if he'd ever thought about donating his rack to a local artist when he died, you know so they could immortalize him. Apparently he didn't find me a-moosing." Said with a wink and a chuckle.

No wonder Travis had a file an inch thick. The bear had a death wish.

"Any idea yet on if this new snake is somehow related to the one Brody killed?" Boris asked.

Master Sergeant Carson shook his head. "We never even found out the name of the one that took you prisoner and then died during your escape."

"They have to be related somehow," Gene interjected. "Because it wasn't a dead man who came to visit me for months after you all managed to flee."

At least Gene managed to say it without growling—or attempting to hit someone. A step in the right direction. When Gene, known by his military brothers as The Ghost, had first come back to Kodiak Point, it had been with the intent to kill all his former army buddies. It seemed someone had anger issues about the fact that, while they'd all escaped, he spent a while longer as the guest of a psychopath.

"The two are most probably related somehow, which might help explain the vendetta against the clan."

"Who cares what their relation is?" Boris grumbled. "I want to stomp his ass and go home to my wife. Preferably with the skin. She and her mother have plans for new purses."

Used to Boris' dry and macabre humor—and yes, she preferred to think of it as humor rather than truth—Jess didn't react. Much.

Having been raised in a small clan on the West

Coast, she'd initially found the wilder nature of her Alaskan brethren a bit much to take in. In the untamed north, recipes still abounded where the main ingredient wasn't always basic cattle, pork, chicken, or fish. Welcome to Kodiak Point, where traitors sometimes ended up the main course in a feast.

"Since we know the bastard's here, we should arm ourselves and prepare to head out. We wouldn't want him to get a chance to regroup. Let's hit him while he's still recovering and on the run." Brody bounced on the balls of his feet, eyes glinting with feral eagerness, his wolf excited to get going.

He wasn't alone. All the guys were chafing to go after their target. Exhausted, Jess could only envy their enthusiasm. While she'd finagled a spot on this trip, she wasn't a battle-trained soldier. Given a choice, she would have taken a good night's sleep so they could start out rested in the morning.

Thankfully, the men's old sergeant took her side without even knowing it. However, his reasons had less to do with beauty rest and more with danger level.

"I'd recommend against heading out so late. Too dangerous."

"Dangerous how?" Brody asked.

"The rebels have been nagging at our troops real bad lately. It's like they know when we're coming. They're hard enough to spot in the daytime, but at night, you can't see fuck all. Not to mention, in the dark, you won't see any traps they might have laid. You gotta watch for landmines along with ambushes."

"Dark or light, I'd say the danger level is high."

"True, but then there's the fact you've already been attacked once today, you just arrived, and judging by the circles under some eyes, you're jet-lagged. Which means you're not functioning at 100 percent, which out here can get you killed. You're better off getting a good night's sleep and waiting for daylight. We'll head out first thing in the morning."

Jess could have hugged the old guy. A night's rest sounded heavenly.

A bell clanged before Brody could argue any further with the master sergeant.

Travis grinned as he announced—with a hopeful glint in his eye—"Dinner!"

Actually the bell was a test of the perimeter security system, which led to a crestfallen bear who grumbled he had a rumble in his tummy. Boris told him he could eat a knuckle sandwich if he didn't stop his bellyaching.

Travis asked if it came with mustard.

Gene threatened to eat them both if they got in a fight, while Brody conversed with Layla in a corner.

Welcome to camp life where sticking four alpha-tendency males in one tent meant too much testosterone and the possibility of fists flying.

To the sound of soft bickering, Jess drifted off to sleep, but it wasn't a restful one. In her dreams—more like nightmares—she soared as a hawk, free in a bright blue sky until a dark swarm converged. A mob of ravens, each bearing a cold blue gaze, chased her, nipping at her tail feathers with their beaks as she coasted the aerial drafts, tiring her until she plummeted.

Down. Down. Down.

In a lethal spiral, she flailed, trying to control her deadly descent. The ground rushing to meet her.

Thump.

She hit the hard floor, only narrowly missing her nose because her hands broke her fall. Instantly, she woke, groaned because of the rudeness of it, and hoped no one noticed her ignoble dismount from her bed. A hope dashed.

Head turned sideways, she opened her eyes and

bit her tongue, lest she squeal at the upside down visage dangling from the bed alongside hers.

Brown eyes peered at her, the corners crinkled with mirth. "You know," Travis said conversationally, "most people prefer to get out of bed on their feet, not their face."

"Why bother standing when I thought I'd do some pushups first to get the blood flowing?" she quipped, pumping a few. When embarrassed, nonchalance always provided a great fallback.

A tsking sound escaped his pursed—and very nice, as well as too close—lips. "Liar," he chided. "Although it is a great cover. I'll have to remember it the next time my handsome mug hits the floor."

If she were one of the guys, she might have refuted his handsome claim, but she'd already fibbed once. "Maybe if you behaved and didn't do things to end up on the floor, you wouldn't need a cover," she replied, dropping her pretense at pushups so she could perch on her cot.

"Behave? But that would ruin all my fun." He looked and sounded appalled, which made her laugh.

Actually, a lot of things Travis did made her laugh, crack a smile, and feel good. While many saw him as a clown—and in some ways he was—his wasn't a malicious kind of humor, but a playful one. Travis never saw the negative. He never let adversity bring him down. He also never passed up a chance to tease, hence his numerous visits to the infirmary. Yet he never resented the damage he took. Never complained. And he was never truly grievously hurt.

Much as the guys liked to threaten him and, in some cases, hit him, they also cared for the grizzly. One might compare him and his antics to the pesky little brother that drove them insane but that they'd defend with their last breath.

As for her, he was the ray of sunshine in what was a bleak life. A teddy bear who just had to exist to make her smile. A man who made her want—

Ack. What was with her? Smiling at Travis, admiring his smile, getting all warm and fuzzy inside. *Snap out of it.* She wasn't here on a holiday, nor had she come to flirt. Theirs was a serious mission, hers doubly so, as she tried to find a resolution to her future.

Kill the raven, solve the problem.

Such a simple solution from her hawk, but Jess liked to think she was a tad more civilized. But she couldn't deny the temptation was there to let her avian side take care of matters. Or to drug Frederick senseless, drag his ass out to the desert, stake him in the sun, dribble honey on him, and let nature take its course.

See, no need for her to perpetrate violence when she could count on the wild to do its thing.

But enough plotting. Gritty-eyed or not, time to see if anything interesting occurred while she slumbered. Or not.

It seemed she wasn't the only one who'd taken advantage of the down time they had before dinner. All around, she noted signs of the beds being used, the sheets rumpled. A few cots over, Boris snored loudly on his. It didn't go unnoticed.

A certain grizzly, with a naughty look in his eyes, held a finger to his lips as he snuck over to Boris' side. Surely she wouldn't sit still and let him intentionally start trouble?

Or maybe she would.

To stem any giggles, she slapped a hand over her mouth when Travis tiptoed over to the moose, shaking a can of shaving cream. Before he could spray, Boris' hand shot out and gripped his wrist.

"Do it and die."

"Boris, old buddy, old pal, surely you aren't

accusing me of doing something nefarious like say filling your palm full of shaving cream and then tickling your nose so you slapped it in your face?" Deadly long lashes fluttered in mock innocence.

With a growl—which was truly impressive given Boris was a moose—the big man vaulted off his cot, but Travis was already fleeing from the tent laughing. "Catch me if you can, old man."

"I am not old," Boris bellowed, taking off after him.

With a sigh, a smile, and a shake of her head, Jess watched them go.

Boys!

Travis knew how to push Boris' buttons, and Boris just couldn't help reacting. It was as predictable as the sun rising every day.

"Sometimes that boy is smarter than I give him credit for," Gene remarked.

She jumped, startled at how silently he'd come alongside her. The man truly had a gift for sneaking. But it was his words that had her asking, "How is taunting Boris smart?" Last she'd heard from the medical society, inviting concussions was anything but.

"It's smart because anyone watching will see exactly what you did, a rascally cub antagonizing his elder."

"I still don't get it."

"What do you think they're doing right now?" Gene asked.

Her brow knit in a frown. "Doing? I'd imagine racing around camp until Boris corners Travis and knocks him silly."

A hint of a smile teased his lips. "You got that partially right. Yes, they are whipping around, Travis antagonizing Boris. Probably making some stupid moose joke—like telling Boris to watch out for moose-quitos."

"Or asking him to hold his radio so he can get better reception from his big antlers."

"Exactly. Two outsiders screwing around. No biggie. No threat. No one pays them much of a second glance unless it's to laugh. But meanwhile, Travis and Boris are getting an eyeful."

"An eyeful of what?"

"Let me ask you. If you were to leave this tent and try to wander off, unescorted, peeking around, what do you think would happen?"

Her still muddy mind began to grasp where he was going with this. "More than likely, I'd get escorted back here or to a common area."

"Bingo."

"But Travis and Boris aren't sauntering, they playing a game of chase. Running all over and more than likely through places considered off-limits to strangers. A great plan, except how do you know that's what they're actually doing? I mean, I know Travis. He lives to drive Boris nuts. What makes you think this is part of some subtle plot to spy?"

"Like I said, behind the boy's playful nature hides a smart mind. He might not choose to show it to the world, but he grasps things. Perhaps if you weren't so busy trying to ignore what's in front of you, you'd see the truth."

With those enigmatic words, Gene slipped away, off to scare some other poor, unsuspecting soul while leaving her with food for thought.

She'd never stopped to consider Travis' actions as anything more than mischief and a tendency to blurt things he shouldn't. She vowed to pay closer attention and see if Gene's observation held any weight because she had her doubts.

Doubts she needed to hold on to because a playful Travis always getting into trouble was easier to keep at bay than an intelligent one who did things to attain a certain result. *Although I don't know what's smart about getting stung by a hundred bees just because he craved some fresh honey.*

Speaking of food, dinnertime arrived. While there was no bell to announce it, as they resided in a military installation, meals were at specified times.

Joining Layla and Brody, Jess went with them to a tent that loomed larger than the rest. As they stepped through the flap, Jess took a peek around.

The large canteen held many tables and benches, mostly empty. Given the number of barrack tents she'd seen, Jess couldn't help but frown. "Where is everyone?"

Had they arrived amidst a big operation?

Brody, who apparently spent some of the time between their arrival and dinner elsewhere, had the answer. "Missing or dead. According to Sarge, their numbers started getting hammered hard in the last year and a half. At first they thought troops might be deserting as they vanished in single digits. The weak ones as Sarge called them."

"AWOL is the common consensus." Boris, who'd arrived before them, didn't peer back at them as he replied. He paid more attention to the ladled mashed potatoes and brown, gravy-soaked lump that passed as meat. The peas on the other hand were a bright green—too bright. But at least the pudding appeared normal.

"That's one possibility," Brody conceded. "No one's sure what happened to those fellows, only that they just never came back."

"You said at first. What about now?" Jess asked.

"The siphon of troops stopped at one point, and that's when the skirmishes began. As part of keeping the area clear of rebel forces, the camp began sending out groups of soldiers, half of them shifter, the other half human, to sweep the hills and nearby villages. Providing aid where needed, a visible presence to deter the enemy from encroaching and trying to terrorize folk into joining their cause. It used to be a pretty simple gig with only the occasional resistance. But all that changed about six months ago. Now Sarge says they can't leave the base at all without some kind of incident. Sometimes it's benign, like a broken-down engine or a flat tire. Other times it's outright war where the soldiers get gunned down or hit a hidden landmine."

"Each time?"

Brody nodded.

"And yet, knowing this, they sent only three soldiers to meet us."

"Bingo." Gene drawled. "And I might add, of those three soldiers, two were wet behind the ear while the other didn't have any weapons to arm us."

"Something's not right," Boris grunted in between mouthfuls.

"Why invite us in if they're planning to sabotage? They could have just as easily refused us and let us stumble around getting equipped on our own," Jess said, playing devil's advocate.

"According to Sarge, they hoped by keeping things low key, we'd attract no notice."

"I'd say that failed," was Boris' dry retort.

"How many people knew we were even coming?" Jess asked.

"Not many."

Brow furrowed, Jess tried to make sense of it and could only come up with one conclusion. "Someone in the camp is feeding the rebels information."

At her reply, Gene nodded. "Bingo again. But the question is, who? Sarge says they've tightened up security. The soldiers don't know where they're going or when until the moment they leave camp. Communication is only done under supervision. They've made it so that no unauthorized personnel can exit or enter. Yet the enemy always seems to know their every move, and more disturbing, lately there's been incidents in camp."

"What kind of incidents?" Travis asked, of course folding his lanky frame into the seat across from her. A whole table to sit at and he would choose the one that forced him into her line of sight.

But at least he's willing to sit with me.

A certain cowardly raven hadn't yet dared a reappearance since their arrival in camp, which, to her surprise, didn't truly bother her. After his last nasty words, and demeanor, she found herself at a loss as to what to do about him.

The boy she married just no longer existed. On the tarmac she'd faced a stranger. A hateful one at that.

To think one of my plans when I came over here was to drag him back and use him to get pregnant.

The very idea now made her ill. Did she really want a child with Freddie?

No.

She didn't want him in her life. She never wanted to set eyes on him again. Ever. At this point, she doubted if she'd care if he fell victim to one of the rebel ambushes. In a sense, his demise would provide relief, an awful thing to think—wish for—and yet, she felt no remorse.

Given her emotions in his regard, she really had to wonder about the whole mating thing for life. Could it be that something she'd taken as an unbreakable truth all her life was more myth than reality?

What would happen if she divorced Freddie and chose to move on?

History said she couldn't, but nothing ever explained what would happen if she did. Gene had raised some valid points when he asked if breaking the bond would kill her. Having never known someone who had, she really couldn't reply. As a doctor, she heard her fair share of old wives tales—chicken soup for the ill, feed a fever, starve a cold—was she a victim of an urban legend or, in this case, a shifter one?

My attraction to Travis would certainly make more sense then. Because logic dictated if she were truly mated, then she should never crave another. It certainly was something to ponder. A divorce would prove a much simpler thing to accomplish than praying for Freddy to drop dead—or to constantly peer over her shoulder wondering if her husband plotted her demise. Something she wouldn't put past him since their ugly confrontation.

Her train of thought derailed as Master Sergeant Carson sat down with them, his sudden arrival quelling the hushed conversations flowing around her.

"Hope I'm not interrupting," the older man said.

As if he cared. Jess got the impression he said it more out of expected courtesy.

"Nope, sir. Not at all," Travis replied with a genial smile.

"Sir? Don't call me, sir, cub. I'm Master Sergeant. You will address me as such. Is that understood?" he barked.

The rebuke took her aback.

Properly chastised, Travis straightened in his seat. "Yes, Master Sergeant."

"That's better. You're on a military base now, and as such, we got certain rules to follow, even with guests. Properly addressing those by their rank is one of them. But I guess I'll have to cut you a little slack given you're not a true recruit. Although, from what I hear, my boys brought you along in the hopes of toughening you up."

Used to Travis' usual cockiness, she expected a rebuttal. If there was one thing Travis excelled at, it was being tough. The bear knew how to take a licking and keep on smiling.

It surprised her to hear him say, "I'd like that,

Master Sergeant. I've always looked up to the guys who served under you, and if you can teach me a fraction of what they know, I'd appreciate it."

Travis showing respect? She'd have to check him later for signs of concussion or brain damage. Perhaps Boris had played a little too rough when he caught him during their mini spy run earlier.

"Unfortunately, we won't have much time, what with us leaving in the morning and all, but I'm sure we could arrange a little something after dinner."

Boris nudged Gene. "This should be good," he muttered.

"Wager on it?" Gene let a smile ghost his lips.

"We don't even know who his opponent is going to be."

"What makes you think there's even going to be a fight?" Jess asked, a question apparently the whole table heard, or so she assumed given all the guys burst out laughing.

"Of course he's going to test Travis' skills with a fight. How else can he judge where he needs help in his training?"

"A hundred bucks says the boy holds his own," Gene announced.

Boris snorted. "Not against an experienced fellow, which is what I'll bet the master sergeant will pit him against."

"He's got a hard skull. I think he can handle a few knocks to it."

"Dude, what makes you think I'll get hit in the head?" Travis interjected, his tone offended, but his smile amused and his eyes alight with excitement.

Jess wanted to bang her head off the table.

Boys. Couldn't they do anything that didn't involve violence?

Apparently not, because no sooner were the trays

dumped and placed in a bin for the kitchen staff to wash than they were heading outside to a training area conveniently placed close to the medical tents, which were distinguished by their large red crosses.

It didn't take long before a few handfuls of men gathered to line the edge of the dirt-packed area. Even someone without medical knowledge would have noted the brownish stains—dried blood—soaked into the ground, and her nose twitched at the acrid stench comprised of the sweat of hundreds of men who'd bled and perspired. Only someone truly naïve with all these clues would not expect something truly violent and savage.

What did surprise her was Freddie showed up. Standing across from her and the group from Kodiak Point, he slouched against a post, cigarette once again hanging from his mouth, his gaze dark and brooding.

A shiver went through her. Her hawk ruffled its mental feathers. It wouldn't allow them to be intimidated.

Freddie didn't like her being there? Too bad. She'd spent too long allowing him to play his hurtful game. Time to step into his comfort zone and rattle things around.

The master sergeant stepped into the middle of the makeshift arena, and at his appearance, the low buzz of conversation died off. "So, boys, as you might have noticed, we got some visitors. Most of them, some soldiers I trained. A tough bunch if I say so myself."

"Not tougher than you, Master Sergeant," one ass-kisser called from the crowd. A rumble of laughter accompanied his statement.

"Not much is tougher than my leathery skin, but if any folk come close, then it's these guys. But they're not the reason we're here. They brought along a new fellow, a cub, one could say, among bears."

A subtle verbal comparison that the humans

wouldn't grasp, but the shifters in the watching crowd did.

"What do you say we see what this boy's got?"

As expected, the men jeered and grunted in approval.

"Are you sure you want to play?" the old rhino asked Travis.

"Heck yeah, Master Sergeant. I'm always looking for ways to improve, and besides, I think it's time my teachers"—he shot a quick glance at Brody and the rest—"saw their lessons at play."

With his trademark grin, Travis stripped off his shirt and brazenly tossed it at her feet. As if she'd catch it. It smacked too much of a token given to someone of the opposite sex before a joust. Except in this case, instead of a maiden bestowing her favor, it was Travis more or less tossing down a gauntlet.

Maybe Freddie wouldn't notice. Hard to tell, as his expression never wavered.

"I like your enthusiasm, boy. So who's going to be first to show him what he's missing not enlisting in the military?" Several hands shot in the air. The master sergeant pointed at one. "Private Corbin, get your lazy butt in here and start things off, would you?"

The first round pitted a human against Travis. Not even close to a fair matchup. Travis didn't even break a sweat knocking the poor guy out.

The groggy soldier no sooner hit the ground than he was carried out of the makeshift ring.

Next to step into the makeshift ring, a feline shifter. Light on his feet, he lasted a bit longer and proved quick with the punches. Nothing Travis couldn't handle. A few hits landed, not enough to rock the grizzly. Travis, with his longer reach and solid strength behind each throw, soon had the Sergeant calling an end to that match.

As Travis gulped down some water—the muscles in his throat working, not that she paid much mind, her eyes inadvertently strayed to his glistening torso despite how many times she chastised herself—the rhino stepped back out into the arena.

"I see you've got some skill, boy. Let's see how you do against someone with real talent. Master Corporal Weller, would you show the boy what you've learned."

With a malicious leer, Freddie cracked his knuckles and stepped on the field. "Of course, Master Sergeant."

Jess could have groaned. Especially when Gene, who up until now had backed Travis, muttered in a low voice, "Fuck. There goes my hundred bucks."

Chapter Ten

Bouncing on the balls of his feet, just warming up, Travis ignored the mutters as Frederick took a position in the fighting ring.

A part of Travis understood he'd been set up, the previous matches just a precursor for the main event. After all, what were the chances the rhino would pair him with the one person he most longed to fight?

I get to hit him. I get to hit him.

Yes, the idea filled him with a childish glee. He'd wanted to smack that smug prick since he'd laid eyes on him.

Jealousy issues? Damn straight. It didn't matter that Travis was the interloper looking to steal Jess from her mate. Frederick was a dick, one who didn't deserve a wonderful woman like Jess.

I'm going to take you down a peg or two, raven.

At least he wanted to. Thankfully not just his bear and jealous instinct were making his decisions. A part of him realized this upcoming fight posed a dilemma.

For example, if Travis took out his bottled frustration on the raven—and it should be noted he had several years' worth—he could cause some serious damage. Cocky? Damn straight.

He noted many in the crowd, even his own crew, harbored some doubt in their eyes. Wouldn't he love to show them what he was truly capable of? What he'd hidden over the years?

To deny he'd get satisfaction out of pummeling Frederick's face wasn't in him, nor did he worry about being punished if he did. The whole purpose of this exercise, which he'd realized early on, was to put him in his place. To make him feel inadequate.

Obviously they didn't know him well. As if that would work. Travis never allowed anyone to bring him down. He'd long ago made himself a promise to only ever show a positive face. *Never let them see you cry.* Crying was a weakness. As was whining. And, in this case, losing.

However enjoyable, beating the hell out of Doc's hubby could cause issues, not with the guys egging him on, but with Jess.

How would she take it if he took Frederick down? Would she thank him, maybe with a kiss when they got out of sight? Hell, he'd even settle for a wink.

Or would she get mad at him and smother Freddie in attention as she tended his wounds—and if Travis had a say, Frederick would leave this arena hurting.

He wished he knew what to do. *What's the right choice?*

The answer hadn't yet come to him, and the time to wonder about it passed as the raven, now shirtless and with cold intent in his eyes, came at him, fists swinging.

Easy enough to block, but Travis didn't go on the offensive, not yet. First he wanted to gauge the mood of the crowd. He sent out a little jab, right under Frederick's arm and connected with the left side of his rib cage. The birdman let out a grunt.

Hit.

Just not a good enough one apparently.

His own side mocked him.

"I taught you better than that," Boris hollered.

"Get him in a headlock, Master Corporal, and give him a noogie," Brody countered with a grin. The man was such a joker.

"Stop crushing on the bird and give him something harder than love taps," grumbled Gene.

He seemed to have approval from them to beat on Frederick. Awesome.

As for the watching soldiers, they didn't react much when Frederick landed blows, but when Travis managed to sneak a few past the raven's guard, they smirked, and a few openly jeered.

"About time someone bruised pretty boy's face."

"Take him down a notch."

It seemed dear old Freddie wasn't especially well loved by his peers. However the more important question was, did Jess still care for him?

Given her tight lips, crossed arms, and silence from the sidelines, he couldn't tell.

A bull rush from the raven had Travis opening his arms to clasp the other man to him.

As they hugged to Boris yelling, "Get a room," Freddie whispered, "I know you've been eyeballing my wife."

Travis, not known for his subtlety, said, "I'd bang her if she'd let me."

You'd think a man finding out his wife wasn't cheating would have shown some appreciation, and Freddie did of a sorts. With a snarl—which surprised Travis, who expected a caw, à la Poe—looped a leg around Travis' and took him to the ground.

"Let's see how much she likes you once I scramble your pretty face."

"Are you flirting with me?" Travis replied a moment before they hit the ground with a thump.

"You annoying little prick. I'm going to fucking maim you."

"First off, let's get one thing straight. There ain't nothing little about my junk. And two, we'll see who's doing the maiming. I'm in the mood for some turkey."

Inciting, intentional, and totally fun. Blood coursed through his veins, energizing him as he rolled around in a scuffle of limbs, fists, and more whispered taunts.

Travis was having a wonderful time.

As Frederick managed to pin Travis under him, a forearm pressed against his throat, he growled. "I'm going to stake you out in the desert and let the vultures shred the skin from your bones."

A serious threat indeed, which meant Travis felt justified in saying, "I'm wondering how many pies I can make with you. The poem says four and twenty."

"That was blackbirds, and they were baked into one pie."

"Well, that makes no sense. Given your size, that would be a much-too-large pie. I mean, how would you even cook the thing? Ma has an industrial-sized oven, but even she couldn't handle roasting your carcass. Unless we strung you on a pole over an open fire." Travis kept his tone conversational while, at the same time, preventing the bird from choking him. He also managed to loop his leg around the guy and prepared to make his move.

Frederick pressed down harder. "You're a sick little fucker. Who the hell jokes about eating folk?"

"Hunter's first rule. Don't waste what you kill." With those words, Travis sent Frederick flying over his head to hit the ground with a thump. As he sprang to his feet, ready to go mete out some meat tenderizing, he caught Brody's slight headshake.

Damn.

He understood the message loud and clear. He had to let Frederick live. And given Brody's twitch of an eyebrow, he'd have to pretend to lose.

In front of Jess and everyone.

How ego crushing.

More like nose crunching.

Ow!

It irked his bear that he had to fake fatigue and incompetence to let the bird get the upper hand, but that irritation faded as he caught sight of Jess' face. Whilst she might not have minded Freddie getting smacked around, her eyes told a whole other story now.

Crunch.

The left hook sent him staggering to the ground, where he kept one eye trained on Jess. Yup. She flinched.

Or, as his elation screamed inside him, *she cares!*

Unfortunately, a certain pesky husband noticed it too. And thus did the real beating begin.

Chapter Eleven

Why is no one stopping this?

It took her biting an inner cheek to stop herself from crying out as the fight took a nasty turn.

When it first began, it seemed as if Travis would handily win against all the soldiers thrown at him. He dodged, with ease, the almost sluggish throws of first the human then the shifter. The few blows that did land didn't even stagger him. But that was before he found himself paired with a glowering Freddie.

As soon as her husband stepped in the makeshift ring with Travis, it didn't take a genius to predict trouble. The doctor in her definitely expected bruises and blood, maybe even broken bones.

Or had she, like others, not put enough faith in Travis?

The beginning of the sparring match had Frederick and Travis evenly matched. An almost equal number of punches hit and they wrestled for the upper hand.

She could also catch their lips moving, just not what they said, the noise from those watching and expressing themselves with vocal taunts, drowning their words. Although, judging by Travis' grin and Freddie's scowling expression, she could guess.

He's taunting him. And landing with his barbs if Freddie's reaction was a gauge.

When Travis flung Freddie off him and sprang to his feet, looking as spry as when he started, she began to think all would end well—for Travis at any rate. However that became the point things fell apart. Either Freddie had held back before or Travis lost his rhythm because, suddenly, punches he'd defended against before landed.

A bit of blood flowed as skin split under abusing knuckles. A certain bear's eyes took on a dazed expression. The thud of flesh hitting, bruising, impacting could be heard over the cheers and jeers of those watching.

He's hurting him. Someone step in. Stop this. Do something.

She wanted to cry out, to put a halt to this brutal madness, but a lone female voice amidst all this testosterone? Even she knew better than to speak out.

She turned to Brody to ask him to intervene, only to frown in confusion as she noted him placing a hand on Boris' arm. The small gesture was enough to keep the moose from charging in, but he obviously bristled at the unfolding beating.

Brody was allowing it. Condoning it. But why?

What purpose could be served in the systematic beating? It was savage. Brutal. What had started out as a test of Travis' skills had devolved into something dark.

How could anyone condone the unnecessary violence Freddie dished out? Then again, it wasn't that Brody actively condoned it, but more that he allowed it. Watched it. His keen eyes noted everything from the battle on the field to those who egged the combatants on and saw nothing amiss.

Surely she wasn't alone in thinking this had gone far enough? She peeked to Layla and couldn't help a shiver. Her friend struggled to control her otherness, but still, some of Layla's hair escaped her control and floated in a staticky halo. Ready to call forth what in this arid place? The camp rats or the cats used to cull their population?

Nothing as it turned out. Brody spotted her and said something to her in a low tone. While Layla grimaced, the hum that emanated from her dissipated.

As for the master sergeant, he watched the brutal fight with a placid expression that she found unsettling. He didn't seem to react at all to the fact Travis was getting his ass handed to him. Had he planned this all along to prove something?

Then it was as if a switch was flipped, or Brody gave a signal, because with the subtlest nod at Travis, the grizzly suddenly went from victim to aggressor.

One moment, Freddie hammered at him, and the next Travis not only regained his feet, but he sent the raven on the defensive, his quick jabs not enough to knock Freddie out—not the way he danced around—but it changed the tone of the fight.

The raucous yells of the crowd grew louder as the underdog—erm, bear—gained the upper hand. Punch. Kick.

When one good shot hit Freddie's jaw with a satisfying thud that had him staggering and sinking to the ground on his knees, blinking crossed eyes, the master sergeant finally called it done.

"That's enough for tonight, boys. We wouldn't want to waste all our energy on training. We need to keep ourselves in shape in case those rebels try something."

With the entertainment at an end, the watching soldiers dispersed, but not the crew from Kodiak Point or the rhino.

As their clan beta made his way to Travis, the master sergeant halted Brody. "I know you and your boys are probably tired, but I wondering if maybe we should have a mini meeting in my tent? I was thinking we should go over a few more details before we head out in the morning."

"Sounds good," Brody said, shooting a look at Boris and Gene. They fell in behind the leader of their mission.

As Brody sidled past Jess, he muttered low

enough for only her to hear, "Patch up the bear, would you, and keep him occupied until we're done."

A part of her wanted to protest she should hear what the rhino had to say, but a stronger part of her wanted to rush to Travis' side and check the extent of his injuries.

But her path was blocked by a certain raven.

"In a hurry, *wife*?" Freddie's mocking inflection forced her to meet his cold gaze.

"Get out of my way. I have a clan member to attend to."

"What, no wifely concern over my possible wounds? No tender loving care for your dear husband?"

"We both know you deserved it after what you did to Travis. That was uncalled for."

"Was it? Last I heard a husband had the right to retaliate against those who would poach on his turf."

She snorted. "First off, there is nothing between Travis and me. Second, you lost all rights the moment you stepped out on me. Given your number of infidelities, you've got a lot of nerve."

"And little patience. So don't push me, or you'll find your stay here going from unpleasant to short." With that threat, he stalked off.

With her path clear, Jess frowned as she noted Travis gone from the makeshift fighting ring. A glance around showed Layla and the rest of the clan gone too. All that remained was one cat. A cat sitting there staring at her, a skinny, orange-striped cat who was totally plotting how he was going to sit on her chest while she slept and suck the life from her, cat.

She blinked and kept a threatening shiver under control.

Okay, so she wasn't entirely alone. Layla obviously had *touched* the feline. "You waiting for something, kitty?" she said, feeling only slightly weird for speaking to it.

With a swish of its tail, the tabby stood and slunk off between the tents, guiding her to the one she shared with the others.

As she neared, she could hear voices.

"I really should go check on her. She shouldn't be alone with that prick."

How utterly man-ish of Travis to assume she needed protection. Cute too.

"She is not alone. I have eyes on her."

"Eyes won't keep her safe. And no offense, but none of your minions in camp are a match for the guy."

"I wouldn't be so sure of that," Layla said in a dulcet voice, her accent lilting the words. "Nor would I mock my abilities considering I could, within moments, swarm you with eight-legged, a zillion-eyeballed, hairy spiders."

Before Layla could enact her threat on a suddenly silent bear, Jess entered and found Layla standing by a bunk. She seemed intent on preventing Mr. Paw-in-his-mouth from moving. It seemed a certain bear had a fear when it came to arachnids, seeing as how he'd tucked his feet onto the cot as he peered anxiously at the floor.

Jess also eyed the space under the bunks. *Hairy spiders?* Shudder. Some things were best fumigated.

"You can stop baiting each other," Jess announced. "I'm here. Safe and sound. While your concern is touching, I'm not afraid of Freddie."

Caught in a sham of a marriage with him, was there really anything worse he could do to her?

He might try and kill me.

He could try. He wouldn't find Jess so easy to take out. Putting up with his behavior didn't mean she'd simply lay down and die.

"Ah, good, you're here." Layla greeted her with a smile. "If you don't mind keeping Travis company, I'm going to commune with nature for a bit. Now that I'm fed, I'm feeling a touch energetic. I swear, I thought I'd wither away from lack of food." Layla was a girl who never missed a meal, and snacked often, or so Jess noticed. A byproduct perhaps of the energy she expended using her power. "I want to see what's around the camp."

"Does Brody know you're going exploring?" Jess asked. In other words, would he lose his freaking mind if he came back and discovered his wife had gone wandering?

"He's the one who suggested it. And if you're worried about my safety, don't be. I'm armed courtesy of Boris and wearing a vest." She flashed some Kevlar. "Brody's idea. My mate can be very protective. Which is silly, my little friends are keeping an eye. If anyone comes near me, I'll know, and so will Brody."

"But will they catch a sniper?"

"That's what my eyes in the sky are for," Layla replied with a smile. "Lots of vultures in these parts. And I don't plan to go far, just enough that I can say *hello* to a few four legged friends in the mountains."

The casual manner with which Layla referred to and used her powers sometimes frightened Jess. The woman controlled animals, and not just one at a time. She could *live* through dozens at once, and Jess would wager, that as Layla practiced and used her ability, she'd only grow stronger. More dangerous. More tempting to those with nefarious intentions.

A good thing Layla had Brody. Not only would he protect his mate from those who might seek to capture and imprison Layla again.

He'll make sure she keeps playing for our side. As much as Jess liked Layla, she couldn't help but be wary of her.

Hair adrift, a hum emanating from her frame, and her eyes taking on an odd cast, Layla left, and Jess breathed a sigh of relief.

"Gotta admit, she's a touch freaky," Travis stated as if reading her thoughts. "But cool."

"Glad she's on our side now because, damn, she's got the potential to be dangerous."

"I think that's one of the things Brody finds sexy about her."

"So you think she's sexy?" Jess asked as she knelt at Travis' side, her eyes scanning the extent of his injuries. The question was wholly inappropriate, especially since it was accompanied by a squirt of jealousy.

"She's okay if you like the exotic type. I'm more partial to redheads myself." No subtlety there.

The heat enflaming her cheeks took her by surprise. When was the last time Jess had blushed over a compliment? It really wasn't something she should encourage.

Look at him. Look at where his crush on me has gotten him. As she dabbed at his wounds, she couldn't help but berate him. "You idiot. Why didn't you stop the fight with Freddie?"

"Why would I do that?"

She gave him a pointed look then poked at a blossoming bruise.

He laughed. "Yeah, he got a few in, but I won."

"After getting your ass handed to you."

"All part of my strategy," he said with a wink.

"A strategy that involved him pummeling you?" She couldn't help a note of incredulity.

Unrepentant as ever, Travis grinned, his swollen lower lip, a temptation she quickly looked away from.

He's hurt. I shouldn't be thinking of kissing his booboos better.

"Hey, the boss thought it was necessary."

"So Brody did order it? But why?"

Travis shrugged. "My guess is he was learning. And I didn't mind because I was learning too," he replied.

"Learning that a beating hurts," was her dry retort.

"Oh, I already knew that. But here's something you don't know. By letting someone go at you and not putting up much of a defense, you end up getting a lesson."

"A lesson in how not to sob for your mommy?"

Her crude jest made him smile.

"Oh please. As if I'd ever do that. My ma would have used her spoon on me herself if she ever heard me begging her to save me. No, the lesson I'm talking about is more of a life experience. How else can you know what you can handle unless you push your limits? In a fight, especially one where you let your opponent have his way, you get to see how your body reacts to certain blows. Teach yourself how to brace for it. You get to see the exact motion they're employing, and you can devise a counter. By experiencing it, I never forget it. Hence, I learn from it. It's how I improve my skills."

"Getting a black eye, fat lip, who knows how many bruises on your ribs, is improvement? I don't buy it. No man lets himself get beaten to a pulp for any reason."

"I do. And I'm glad I did because, while I don't know what Brody spotted, I learned a few things."

"Such as the taste of sand?" By insulting him, she hoped to fight his allure, an allure that multiplied the more she dabbed at the blood on his skin.

As she wiped the traces of battle from him, she couldn't help but note the things she tried to ignore. The smoothness of his flesh. The firmness of his muscle. Even the smell of sweat didn't bother her. On the contrary, she fought a temptation to lick his skin to taste the salt.

"Ma always said dirt might not taste good, but sometimes it did a boy good to get a mouthful of it, for the vitamins you know." He said it with complete seriousness.

"Travis, you do realize your mother was just trying to make you feel better because someone beat the hell out of you."

He winked at her. "Of course I know that. But guess what? It did me good. In the end, all those face rubs in the dirt made me determined to get stronger. You might find this hard to believe, but I used to be a runt of a cub. Shortest and scrawniest of my age group. So you can imagine what happened at school. One day, I decided that just because someone picks on me it doesn't make me weak. I was just untrained. Not having a dad around, I didn't get the same benefit the other boys did. I needed to create ways and scenarios where I could sponge some fatherly advice."

His admission captivated her. How lonely for him growing up. She'd had two parents. Still did. They lived out on the east Canadian coast, in Halifax, Nova Scotia. She saw them a few times a year and spoke every other week to them on the phone. But Travis? He had only his mother, a woman who could cook up a storm but knew nothing about training a grizzly cub to become a predator, or a man.

"What about the other dads? Surely there were a few to help a kid out?"

"You have met my mother, right?" Asked with a wry query.

"Yeah." Betty-Sue was a true matron and ferocious mama bear.

"I love Ma, but she scares the shit out of a lot of the men. None of them dared take me under their paw, lest they incur her wrath."

"And yet she allowed you to get picked on as a kid? That doesn't make sense."

"She might seem scary—"

Jess arched a brow.

He laughed. "Okay really scary, but in her defense, she wanted to do her best by me, which meant letting me fight my own battles. When I'd come home a little banged up, she'd wipe off my wounds, feed me some freshly baked cookies, and say, 'What did you learn this time?' I'd tell her, and then she'd kiss my booboos better."

He gave her a hopeful look.

She ducked her head. *Must not give in. Ignore the big bear eyes. Ignore the hot stud's body. Keep your mind on the job.* And no, that job didn't involve stripping his pants off and making sure all of his organs were functioning. "Seems a little rough," she replied, wiping at a scratch on his upper pec.

"I guess, but it worked. I think. At least it's how I taught myself the skills other boys get from their dads."

She wrinkled her nose. "My dad taught me how to swap out bedpans and sew gashes with tight stitches."

"Just like my ma taught me my manners and the difference between a ma who's happy I remembered to wipe my muddy paws and a ma who isn't afraid to paddle me with a wooden spoon until I remember. Experience, good or bad, teaches us. Especially when it's bad."

"Meaning?" Because she couldn't help but think he was talking something deeper.

"Meaning that you don't need to repeat mistakes. Oh and that you can only win with boldness."

Boldness such as stealing a forbidden kiss.

One long overdue.

His lips pressed against hers, not demanding, but not too shy either. With slowness and sensuality, he embraced her. A thrill of excitement hummed through all her nerves.

Molten blood pumped through her veins, heating her body, bringing it to life.

The beat of her heart quickened, arousing her

senses.

Caught by surprise, her breath caught, afraid to inhale or exhale because each involved a level of intimacy she didn't know if she could handle.

Forget handle. She craved.

As his lips claimed hers softly, she couldn't help but melt. How long since she'd imagined this? How long had she wanted someone to touch her? To bring her alive? To remind her what it meant to be a woman, a woman with needs, wanted by a man who desired her?

I'm tired of waiting and wanting and feeling guilty.

Time to be selfish.

She kissed him back, and she could have sworn the heat between them burst into molten flames.

As his hand cupped the back of her head, cradling it in his palm, her own fingers tangled in the locks of his hair, drawing him closer, inhaling his breath and moaning as he captured hers.

His groan of enjoyment sent a shiver through her, but it was the holler of an outside voice that dumped a bucket of cold reality on her.

"Private, we need another man on the west perimeter."

"Yes, sir."

The intruding voices of strangers snapped her free of the moment and brought clarity back.

What am I doing? I'm a married woman.

Unhappily.

No matter. Nor did it matter Freddie held their vows in contempt. She wasn't the type of woman to forsake her word, or her mate.

Yet I did only a moment ago.

Travis might have initiated the kiss, but she did nothing to stop it. Never once felt an ounce of shame or repugnance. Even now, she yearned to draw him back to her. To do something wrong. Selfish. But oh so pleasurable.

Wrong.

Right.

Who cared? Who'd stop her?

Fuck it. As he looked at her questioningly, for once not speaking but waiting, all his hopes and desires—a desire for her—shining in his eyes, she chose to please herself.

Oh god, it's about time.

She'd spent years unfulfilled and yearning for this moment. Damned if she'd let a piece of paper that meant nothing but misery dictate what she could or shouldn't do.

At their renewed kiss, Travis took things a step further. His arms looped around her upper body, pulling her into the solidness of his body, the closest she'd been to a man in years. She couldn't help a sigh of pleasure at the hardness of his frame, the evidence of his arousal—*an attraction to me!*—pressing against her lower belly.

Throbbing and insistent.

Oh god. I really shouldn't. We shouldn't. I want to. I need to.

Need…

"Hey, Doc, you're needed." The words were yelled by someone outside only moments before they entered the tent.

Only seconds between the two actions, yet she'd already yanked herself away from Travis—and his tempting lips. She turned to rummage in the medical kit by her side to give herself a moment to compose herself.

"Are you Dr. Weller?" a stranger asked.

"She is," Travis replied. "What's up?"

Jess took a deep breath and rose while pivoting to view their visitor. While the private might have wondered at her glazed eyes and full red lips—which tingled with aftershocks—he at least hadn't caught her in a compromising situation.

I was lucky.

Lucky that Freddie hadn't walked in.

He might not want her, but his pride wouldn't allow a challenge such as finding another man kissing his wife. Especially not given his evident dislike of Travis.

"You're needed in the master sergeant's tent. Your clan members are ill."

Ill? And yet they'd seemed in fine form when she'd left them not that long ago.

"Take me to them." After slapping the medical kit shut and buckling the clips, she didn't spare Travis a glance as she followed the private. As if the bear would let her go alone.

She was fully aware of his gaze on her as Travis followed at her heels.

The master sergeant's tent had a small crowd gathered around it, which dispersed as she arrived, probably because the rhino barked, "Find him for me. As in yesterday. Move!"

When the master sergeant used his big voice, soldiers scattered.

"What happened?" she asked without preamble. "Where are my clansmen?"

"Inside. As to what happened, I'm not sure. One moment they were fine, the next they were heaving all over the place. Food poisoning I reckon given how sudden it hit them all."

Upset bellies? Puzzled lines creased her forehead. "That seems odd. They've usually got quite solid constitutions."

"Camp food can take getting used to. Or maybe they caught a bug. How the fuck would I know? I got other things to worry about than upset tummies. If you want to know more, check for yourself."

Master sergeant Carson strode away, and she

frowned at his back. Whatever affected her companions, it hadn't touched the rhino. Nor her. She felt fine, and yet she'd eaten the same things at dinner.

Walking into the tent, she was struck hard by the stench of vomit and wine. Ugh. She wished she'd thought to pop on a filtered mask. The place reeked.

At first glance, given the open bottle of wine on the table and the scattered mugs, it seemed like a simple case of over imbibing idiots, something the sarge had left out. Except there were a few oddities.

Shifters took a lot to get drunk, and while they weaved and wobbled until their body metabolized, they rarely got truly hung over to the point of puking.

But oddest of all, she'd seen them less than half an hour or so ago. Not long enough for anyone to get loaded unless they really put their minds to it and chugged.

The strangeness did not prevent her questioning. "Just how much did you drink?" she asked as she shone her penlight in Boris' bloodshot eye since he was closest.

"Not enough," he slurred. "Two glasses."

Only two? Not even the strongest moonshine could have knocked Boris on his ass like this. Not for lack of trying. Boris had been the only contestant left standing last year at the annual Moon Juice Face Off.

Leaning down, she sniffed his breath, but her human olfactory sense wasn't refined enough to detect anything over the fermented grapes.

However, she did have someone who could. "Travis, can you sniff his breath and tell me what you get?"

"Ugh. You do realize that's totally gross?" He protested but still bent over to bring himself closer to the moose who lay on the canvas floor with his eyes closed, his skin an unhealthy shade of gray.

Despite his grimace, Travis inhaled. "Wine. Red

grape. With a hint of… Vanilla custard. A dash of mashed potatoes, overlaid with vomit." He shot her a mocking glance.

She pursed her lips but didn't reply.

He went on. "Almonds."

"Almonds? Are you sure?"

"Are you questioning my nose?" He angled so his mouth was much too close to her ear. "I can smell *everything*."

Smell yes, but not predict. She hip checked him and hoped that the time it took for him to pick himself off the floor was enough for the heat in her cheeks to subside.

With the hint Travis gave her, she quickly checked the others to confirm her hypothesis. Once she confirmed it, she knew of only one possible recourse. "I need some B12."

"Is now really the time to worry about them taking their vitamins?"

"I need it to counteract the poison."

"Poison? What poison?" Master sergeant Carson entered the tent while asking.

"Judging by their symptoms, someone fed the guys cyanide."

"Impossible," blustered the rhino.

Trust the bear to take her at her word. Travis asked, "Do you think they did it at dinner?"

She shook her head. "Doubtful or we'd all be sick. Not to mention, it seemed to come on pretty suddenly. I smelled wine. Were you drinking?"

Sergeant Carson straightened. "I might have uncorked a bottle, but I shared it with them, and I'm fine."

"Are you?" she asked, noting his sweating forehead. She leaned up on tiptoe and pressed the back of her hand against his rough skin.

"My stomach might feel a little queasy."

"Did the wine have an almond aftertaste?"

"Yeah, how did you know?" Brody groaned from his spot over a garbage pail, his hair hanging over his forehead, screening his eyes.

"In the past, bitter almonds were a commonly used method of poisoning. Many couldn't differentiate them from the safe sweet ones. It only takes about fifteen or so to induce cyanide poisoning. Crush them and add them to a drink and offer them as a snack…" She waved her hand at the plastic container of them in the middle of the table.

"Someone actually poisoned them? On purpose?" The concept seemed to flummox Travis. "But that means…"

"There's a traitor in camp." Sergeant Carson's lips thinned into a straight line. "I've suspected we had one for a while. It's the only thing that made any sense. How else could the enemy know our every move? Until now, I assumed it was just someone feeding information. But this, an attack within camp? That's beyond blatant. It's fucking treason."

"Who delivered the wine and almonds? We need to question them," Jess said.

"Good luck with that. As soon as the boys here got sick, I was a tad suspicious and sent some soldiers to find the one who brought stuff to my tent."

"So you know who it is?"

"Yeah and you do too," Brody muttered.

It didn't take a genius to connect the dots. "Freddie did this?" For some reason the truth surprised her. Yes, she'd not missed the angry undercurrents between them and between Freddie and Travis. But she would have never expected him to stoop to do something this low. This evil.

"He was the one to deliver the stuff, then leave,"

the master sergeant confirmed. "And now he can't be found."

"But why? Why would he try and poison you? He had to know he'd be caught."

"The hearts of men are dark places capable of anything. In this case, though, I'd say a certain blackbird was lured. I hate to be the bearer of unpleasant news, but your husband has been spending a lot of his down time off base. Doing who knows what and with whom. On his last leave, he disappeared for two weeks."

"He was gone two weeks? But where?" Because he certainly never came home.

"No one knows where he was. He came back and never said a word."

"If you suspected him and knew you had a traitor, then why didn't you arrest him or question him?" Brody asked as he staggered to his feet.

"Because the dirty bird was sly. He was in some of the convoys that were attacked. He even came back injured a few times."

"Giving himself a plausible alibi to keep his cover," Gene mused aloud, already losing his pallor. The men who'd returned to Kodiak Point from war had some of the toughest constitutions Jess had ever seen. It would take more than a little poison to bring them down.

Jess often wondered how their mates handled their special brand of toughness or their mental issues. As a person who dealt with trauma and death on a regular basis—shifters not being the cute and cuddly creatures some might picture—Jess couldn't imagine going home every day to someone haunted by darkness and nightmares.

Perhaps that was why Travis drew her. He lacked that hard edge emanating from the men who'd served during wartime. He still saw life with a joyous enthusiasm that was contagious. He took the punches life dished out and learned from them, or so he claimed. He also never let anything keep him down. He always kept his smile.

He also jumped on the chance to go off and do stupid things. Like volunteer to join a search party for the missing traitor, Freddy.

"I want to be part of the search party that goes looking for him."

The rhino shook his head. "You're still too wet behind the ears. You'll just get in the way."

To Jess' surprise, Boris took Travis' side. "You saw him fight. That's only some of the skills he's been taught. The cub's good to go. I'll vouch for him and make sure he doesn't get into too much trouble."

"Ah, I knew you loved me."

Yeah, Boris loved Travis so much he grabbed him in a headlock and told him to be quiet or he'd rearrange his neck until he could look at his own ass.

"We'll all go," Brody announced. "Just give us a minute to change clothes and clean up, then we'll be ready to head out."

Go? They'd just been poisoned. "You can't go anywhere. You're sick." As the medical expert in the group, it behooved her to make an attempt, even if it was doomed to failure.

"Was sick. I'm already feeling better. I think I threw up most of the almond crap, and my body is purging the rest. By the time we're organized to go, I'll be fine."

"You better be, or I'll have you tied to a bed," Layla announced as she swept into the tent.

"Bait, I thought we were going to keep our bedroom antics private," Brody teased his mate, and she blushed, their relationship still new enough for her to get embarrassed.

"Don't make me get the shock collar back out, Thud," she threatened.

Boris snickered then grimaced. "I think I'd prefer getting Tasered to this feeling."

A crease of concern marred Layla's forehead. "What's this I hear about a poisoning?"

The group quickly brought Layla up to date about what happened. At the end of the tale, her hair was floating and her eyes sparked. "This makes me very, very angry."

"Aren't you the cutest? Just like that little Martian on Bugs Bunny," Brody teased. "I'm fine, sweetheart. It will take more than poison to kill my hairy ass."

Layla snorted. "I'm well aware you have a stomach of iron. I still remember what you ate when we were in the midst of escape fifty-seven. I'm still trying to digest those roots you had me gnaw on. I'm more peeved about all the extra laundry this just created. I hope you're not expecting me to wash that mess." She wrinkled her nose as she pointed to his soiled shirt.

"Where's my sympathy, Bait? I was poisoned." Brody rubbed his belly and tried to look pathetic.

Layla didn't fall for it. "Use a bucket. And wipe with a towel, napkin, something other than your sleeve."

"Most mates would be relieved their lover didn't die."

"Fine. I'm glad you're alive." Sarcastically said, but Jess could read between the lines, sensing the teasing was a mask for the worry—and the deep anger. It didn't take a genius to note Layla struggled to keep her emotions in check. It was evident in her stiff posture, the turbulence in her violet eyes, and the fact that her hair danced from an invisible wind. Most uncanny of all, the air in the tent hummed, as if imbued with energy, an otherness that just chilled a person.

"Since there's no talking you out of it, then we'll meet by the gate at—" The rhino checked his watch. "Twenty-two hundred hours."

Given what they'd been told earlier, Jess couldn't help but ask, "What happened to not going out at night? I thought it was too dangerous."

"Plans have changed. We can't allow Weller to get too far ahead, or we might never catch him."

Good point and, really, given the camp proved less than secure, night or day, did it matter when they left? "I'll need to grab some supplies if that's okay so I can repack my med kit." She'd gone through a lot of gauze and antiseptic wipes during her tending of Travis.

"Twenty-two hundred it is. Sweetheart, can we have a word?" Brody ushered Layla out while the rest of them filed out after.

Boris and Gene strode off to the left in order to quickly hit the shower tent and sluice the distinctive smell of sickness from their body. Jess went in the opposite direction because she wanted to hit the field hospital. She wanted a full kit for this trip, plus she intended to grab some B12 to administer to those who'd ingested the poison. It would hopefully help to bind any remaining cyanide in their bodies and expel it safely. Or so a Google search on cyanide poisoning indicated as she tapped away on her satellite phone.

She had a silent shadow as she walked and typed. Travis, who'd not contributed to the conversation, waited until they got out of sight before he mistakenly tried to tell her what to do. "You don't have to go on this trip. Actually, I think it would be better if you stayed here."

She halted between a pair of dark tents, not sensing anyone nearby, which gave them a measure of privacy. "Are you giving me an order?"

"No. You can do what you like. I'm more hoping you'll take my advice and stay where it's safe. I've got a bad feeling about this."

Immediately, she reached out to feel his forehead. His warm skin didn't show hints of cold sweat or a fever.

He caught her hand before she could snatch it back. "I'm not sick. I'm talking more about a gut reaction. We're going after a lunatic, capable of anything. You could get hurt."

His concern coiled around her warmly. "As could you, and everyone else who's going. I understand it's going to be dangerous, but I refuse to stay behind while you hunt my husband down. This is my clan he hurt. Mine. He's a traitor to our kind. My mate or not, I can't ignore what he's done." Because in the shifter world, they didn't show mercy to those who intentionally set out to hurt their own. They didn't get caught up in lengthy due process with lawyers and other stalling tactics. Guilty was punished. Swiftly. And if the crime was vile enough, there were no second chances.

A low rumble vibrated from Travis. "Don't call him that."

"What? My mate?"

Travis grimaced at the word. "He's not your mate. Given what he's done, I think it's pretty obvious Frederick is a lot of things, but your mate? Never."

Given the fact that she could kiss and desire another, she kind of agreed. But in the eyes of her kind, she was still technically married. Hopefully not for long. "I intend to rid myself of that problem once I get my claws on him."

Enough was enough. A woman could handle only so much humiliation before snapping. A hawk could be civilized for only so long before she needed to soar and hunt. Time to let her feral huntress loose.

Not giving Travis a chance to say anything, she brushed past him and prepared herself for their departure.

Getting herself physically ready proved simple. Mentally though? Totally different matter.

Chapter Twelve

Twenty-two hundred hours arrived. However, their planned excursion didn't happen as scheduled.

It seemed treacherous Frederick had left them another surprise in the form of sand in the gas tanks of the vehicles available to them. It took the fuel filters on a few of the vehicles they first started to clue them in. The sergeant called a temporary hold on leaving while they dumped the contaminated gas in the tampered vehicles.

Since this process took time, it meant they got a few hours of sleep. Or, in Travis' case, restless tossing and turning as he relived the kiss with Jess.

He'd expected some level of fireworks. No man could lust after a woman as long as he had and not want to combust. Yet, he could have never truly expected the raging inferno that consumed him.

Every sense ignited as soon as their lips touched. She enthralled him so deeply he almost turned into a wild bear when their kiss was rudely interrupted.

Wouldn't that have gone over well, him chasing after the human private as a grizzly, all because he'd finally gotten somewhere with Jess.

One step forward.

A half-dozen back.

It didn't take a genius to guess she probably regretted it already. Never mind she'd enjoyed it. He knew she'd find an excuse to deny what they shared. What was meant to be.

Didn't she yet grasp and understand that she meant everything to him, which was why it was driving him nuts that she insisted on coming. Bad enough that Boris and Brody appeared a little green around the gills still, but their determination wouldn't let them back down. Gene was in fine form today, if his enthusiastic scowl was anything to go by. The sergeant didn't seem affected at all. Then again, sunglasses could hide a lot.

As for Jess, the circles under her eyes spoke of a sleepless night. Caused by her worry over this mission and who they chased, or dare he hope that he played a small part in her mental turmoil?

As they clambered into the various Jeeps, their rugged four-by-four capability a must for the terrain they would have to travel through, he ensured they shared a seat.

Jess didn't say a word, didn't glance at him once, but she did allow her thigh to rest alongside his. Given the seat provided more than ample space for them both, he took it as a sign.

The miniature convoy of three headed out, waved through the security checkpoint by guards toting rifles.

The sun blazed down on the vehicles, hot and merciless. Despite the helmets and visors they wore, the wind from the open-top vehicle barreled in. The hot air held hints of dust, a fine grit that settled on everything. It tasted especially vile on the tongue, especially when washed down with a sip of tepid water.

The landscape proved different, much different than Alaska. The dry heat and lack of greenery bothered his bear. It grumbled, ill at ease in this strange land. At home, for all that the older guys ribbed him, Travis felt confident, in charge. As a grizzly, he was top of the food chain.

Out here, he didn't know what to expect, or what he might encounter. How would he fare in a battle against a predator born and bred in this exotic place?

While he did miss his mother—so sue him for being a mama's boy—he couldn't deny the exhilaration of the adventure. Despite not knowing what to expect or how things would turn out, Travis hummed with pent-up energy. Adrenaline, a man's best friend—and leading cause of trouble.

Another source of his desire for action resulted from a need for retribution against Frederick. Not because of the fight. Travis never held a grudge over someone who physically bested him. He just worked harder. His need for vengeance wasn't because the cowardly prick had poisoned his best friend, Boris—who would surely mount Travis' head on a wall if he heard himself referred as his BFF in public.

The revenge Travis sought was for Jess. Sweet, hardworking Jess, who deserved so much more out of life than to be chained to an asshat who not only didn't appreciate her but also betrayed her in every way possible.

There wasn't a clan he knew that would punish Travis for resorting to their wilder moral code, which basically said, strongest wins all.

In the animal kingdom, the strongest male mated the female. In the shifter one, while civility had overwritten many of their roots, this was one that surfaced every now and then.

Of course, I might have to compete for the chance to kill the sucker.

Not bad enough Boris, Brody, and Gene were out to get Frederick, even Jess, sweet, saving-lives Doctor Jess, held murder in her eye.

It totally made her sexier.

The Jeeps jostled and bounced on the rutted road, especially once they left the paved area for a hard-packed dirt one. In an odd stroke of luck, it seemed Frederick's vehicle bore a functioning GPS tracker. Was Travis the only one who thought it odd that Frederick would conveniently give them a road map to his location? Surely the soldier wasn't that stupid?

The rhino sergeant seemed to think so, as he

claimed the devices almost unanimously malfunctioned so the wily raven probably assumed the one in the Jeep he'd stolen didn't work.

Also odd was the seeming careless haste of their travel. For a man who had repeatedly warned of the dangers of ambush and hidden mines, the Sarge seemed more concerned with speed in chasing after Frederick than watching for trouble.

The incident from the day before still fresh in his mind, Travis watched the flowing scenery keenly. His mentor, Boris, had once relayed to him—during a rare moment of bonding after he pounced out of a blind and tackled Travis to the ground—that the key to spotting an ambush was to note what stuck out of place.

In other words, strange glints, out-of-place colors, a lack of natural sounds, easy indications that perhaps required investigation. When Travis wheezed out—because Boris relayed this tidbit while sitting on his chest—that Boris had hidden behind a snow blind, the moose pointed out that Travis had other senses than his eyes. His reply that Boris didn't smell like a predator—being a moose and all—and his bear didn't even register it resulted in him learning that it wasn't just lips that could get chapped. A properly delivered snowjob could chafe the skin on a face too.

He also learned that day that just because an animal didn't bear sharp claws or canine teeth didn't mean they weren't a force to be reckoned with. Even the most benign of creatures could turn feral under the right circumstances and with the right weapon.

With all his lessons in mind, Travis watched. A keen eye on things didn't trigger any alarm bells, and in the front seat of the Jeep, Boris seemed unperturbed, his head leaning back against the headrest.

Nothing untoward happened that morning, and within a few hours, they were in the mountainous foothills. They continued on, dehydrating under the blazing sun despite their constant sips of water.

The heat sapped at his earlier energy. The dusty air, heated and dry, burned the lungs to inhale, yet still they traveled onward, following the flashing dot of a beacon they hoped would lead to their prize.

Late afternoon, the convoy came across the Jeep Frederick had stolen, abandoned and lacking its driver. As if he'd stick around for punishment. This way was actually better. It meant they got to hunt.

His bear practically did a two-step in his head.

As they piled out of the vehicles, a motley crew of shifters, half from Kodiak Point, even more from camp, Travis frowned.

Why did none of the soldiers make a pretense of at least looking for the enemy? They milled around, quiet, sullen. Totally out of character.

Brody, Gene, and the master sergeant, had wandered over to check out the abandoned vehicle. Layla remained seated in her Jeep, head tilted, probably doing her animal whisper thing.

Travis sidled over to Boris and muttered, "Is it me or—"

"There's something wrong with this scenario? There is. I smell a double cross."

Surely not all those soldiers were part of the treachery going on?

"What do we do?" Travis asked. The numbers wouldn't have usually bothered him. Those they faced weren't especially high on the totem pole of strength or cunning; however, no amount of muscle or skill in the world would stop a bullet.

"Do? I'd say that's obvious. We are going to stay alive."

"Well duh. But what's the plan?" Surely the moose had some brilliant strategy.

"I just told you the plan. Don't die."

His first huge treacherous ambush and Boris wanted to wing it. Ah, hell no.

Travis bounced on the balls of his feet. "What about you take the three to the left, I've got the four to the right. On the count of three, we go wild."

"See the problem with that is you're assuming they'll cooperate and stay where they're supposed to. I say, fuck a plan. Plans just make things complicated. Do your best and don't croak. I don't want to have to explain to your mother that I let you kick the bucket on your first overseas mission."

Nothing better happen to him or his mother would brave the afterlife to come find him. Of more concern at the moment than his mother, though, was a certain red-tailed hawk. "What about Jess?" He inclined his head at her where she sat in the Jeep, head bent over her phone again, tapping and searching for who knew what.

"I'd recommend she not die too."

Apparently Jess was paying enough attention to give the moose a thumbs-up and reply, "Gotcha. Good plan."

Good plan? Were they both insane? Okay, Boris was borderline certifiable, but he'd thought Jess level-headed. Where did this teasing side come from? And why did she choose to display it now of all times?

Usually the joker wherever they went, Travis finally grasped how his jocular responses might irritate others in serious situations. "You're both not funny." His own words struck him as ironic, and a grin stretched his lips. If they wanted to treat the situation with levity, then who was he to throw a monkey wrench—or usually in Boris' case, a right hook—into the mix? "By all the hair on my grizzly chin-chin, we'll wing it, hoof it, and paw it. But I'm going on the record right now as saying I get dibs on the fat one. He smells like donuts, and my bear really likes donuts."

"Only if you can get to him first." Boris flashed him a challenging smile.

"Boys!" Jess muttered under her breath. "Always thinking with their bellies."

"So when do we make our move?" Travis asked.

"We don't, at least not until our suspicions are proven correct, which I'm figuring will be anytime now. So hang tight. You'll know when it's time."

Wait?

His inner teddy grumbled. Now that it faced the prospect of a little violent sport and bloodshed, it wasn't content to remain caged. It wanted to make the first move and charge.

But Boris was right. Acting before proof could land them in hot water—the legal kind, not the broth the ladies sometimes had going back home to drop in fresh kills along with vegetables and seasoning.

Damn but I miss Ma's cooking.

As Travis leaned against the hood of the Jeep, attempting a nonchalance he didn't feel, he eyed the soldiers who still clustered together several yards from him. The soft murmur of their voices remained masked by the rumbling engine of the Jeep they'd left running, but he could imagine it, especially since they cast the occasional furtive glance his way.

As for his best bud, Boris? With his hands jammed in his pockets, the moose whistled as he approached Gene, his attempt to look unconcerned and harmless an epic fail as far as Travis was concerned. Who could miss the jaunty swagger, the eager gaze, and the taut readiness of the big man?

Yet it wasn't Gene or Brody who called him on his evident readiness for a fight but the rhino.

"Boy, you look about as subtle as a whore wearing

fishnets, a mini skirt, and a bra in church. I should have known this wild bird chase wouldn't fool you. But it doesn't matter. You're on my turf now, and there ain't no one here to help you."

"I always did like bad odds," Boris riposted. "It makes the win so much sweeter."

"Such misplaced optimism. I thought I taught you better. Soldiers, it's time. Take them. Alive if you can. The master wants them breathing."

Judging by the less-than-shocked miens on Brody's and the other faces, it seemed the fact that the master sergeant was one of the traitors didn't surprise them. The soldiers milling about uselessly snapped to attention, some shedding garments to shift, others aiming their weapons.

Good thing Travis was prepared because, in a blink of an eye, the situation went from boring wait to shit's-hitting-the-fan.

But at least they're not out to kill us. According to the rhino's command at any rate. Alive apparently, though, didn't mean uninjured.

Guns were leveled, most of them the tranquilizing kind, but not all. Quick reflexes saw the folk from his clan moving for cover before the first bullets whistled past.

Adrenaline filled him with an energized rush.

Let me out. His bear practically danced, begging for release. He could so easily picture himself barreling at the threat, roaring a challenge, watching them scatter. But such an act meant leaving Jess exposed and alone. Vulnerable. Unacceptable.

First he had to stash her somewhere safe.

Or not.

A whirl to face her found her already stripping behind the wheel of the Jeep, which acted as a shield from stray missiles.

"I don't think flashing them your gorgeous

breasts will work," he muttered as he hunkered down beside her, although it proved distracting to him. Why was it every time he got a chance to see her naked their lives were in danger?

He did his best to keep his gaze averted.

"I was thinking more along the lines of getting out of the way by taking to the skies."

"And make yourself a tempting target?" He peered at the blue sky, which would highlight her presence, not hide it.

"I'm a target on the ground too, but in the air, at least I can maneuver and use the sun's rays to my advantage. Men blinded by sunspots can't see to shoot."

"How about instead you go get help?" From whom though, he wasn't sure. Had the rhino brought all the traitors with him, or were those remaining back at camp part of his rebellious troop too?

"Getting any kind of aid would take too long, and you know it. Now stop trying to protect me. I can take care of myself. I'm going to soar out of here, and you are going to shift into your furry self and show those bastards how tough a grizzly is."

"Really?"

She wasn't going to try and talk him out of being a badass bear or order him to stay back.

Awesome. Was it possible for him to love her any more? The plan appealed on every one of his levels.

"Tear off an arm or two for me, would you?" Her eyes shone teasingly when she said it, but it was the light kiss across his lips that made him…

A bullet singed past, just skimming his arm, but nicking her.

Unacceptable.

The coppery scent of her blood overcame rational thought.

Rawr!

They hurt my woman.

His bear had only one thought about that.

Kill.

Given Travis was only a passenger as his body morphed in an instant from human to massive grizzly, he didn't argue. Why would he? He agreed with his beast.

No one hurt his Jess and lived to tell.

Of course, his decision might have worked out better were he armed with more than fur and fang. Ooh and claws, mustn't forget the claws.

However, when fighting against those armed with guns? Yeah, not so handy.

A missile impacted his upper shoulder, and another skimmed his thigh before he barreled into the offender. The scream wasn't as satisfying as the crunch when his bear let the shooting human know what he thought of his rifle aim.

But that was just one man down.

Boris, who also seemed to be bleeding and still held his human shape, grinned across a pair of bodies and yelled, "Two for one. Booyah!"

A competition? If Travis could have grinned in his bear shape, he would have—and probably made a nature videographer faint while getting a zillion hits on YouTube.

As it was, he didn't have time to strike any kind of pose because the danger had just begun. As the master sergeant yelled to stop shooting with bullets and use the darts only, Travis noted the numbers against them seemed to have swelled.

Well, that wasn't good for them at least, but on a brighter note, it seemed Jess had gotten away. He spared a quick glance overhead and saw her coasting the aerial wind streams. A sharp caw, one of warning, and a subtle roll of gravel shifting behind him had him ducking, which, given he was a bear, meant dropping to his belly.

The butt end of a rifle whistled overhead.

Try to knock me out, will he?

Travis rolled sideways, crashing into the legs of his attacker.

Pinch.

Ow.

The stinging spot in his shoulder showed a tufted dart. One tranquilizer? No problem.

The second before he took out the Sandman firing his nocturnal missiles? He barely noticed it. Not a yawn.

But he did worry about the guy crouched on the hilly area to his left, kneeling and taking aim at the sky.

There was just one person up there the dick could be aiming for.

More worrisome, even as he began his rush, he knew he wouldn't make it in time before the guy fired.

Rat-tat-tat.

With a grunt, Travis plowed into him. That put an end to the asshole's shooting but not before Travis heard the scream of pain from above.

One of the bullets hit Jess. So he hit the guy—tit for tat—hard enough to knock him out. Then he faced a dilemma. As a bear, he couldn't exactly restrain the guy in case he regained consciousness, and this wasn't the time for sportsmanship.

Travis couldn't help but recall a nugget of advice Boris dispensed—*Sympathy will get you killed. Never leave a murderous enemy at your back. They won't hesitate, and neither should you.*

Not usually one for cold-blooded violence, Travis, the man, closed his inner eyes as his bear did what had to be done. The regret could come later.

He didn't linger over the dead body. A certain hawk was in trouble.

While not plummeting like a rock from the sky,

she was definitely spiraling. He scrambled the rocky face nimbly, his paws and claws gripping the jutting protrusions as he cut at an angle toward where he predicted she'd end up.

It seemed he proved a tempting target. A few more darts in his buttocks sapped his adrenaline, but stubborn will kept him from slowing down.

His mind did at least. His body on the other paw? The drugs coursed through his system, his movements grew sluggish.

He blinked. He teetered. He tottered.

Not good and yet there was nothing he could do.

At the peak of the hill, on a slim ridge, he stumbled and weaved, a drunken beast with no balance. He tumbled right off the far edge and down the side of the incline, leaving Jess to fall, his friends to fight alone, and him to sleep.

Some hero I turned out to be.

Chapter Thirteen

Even though they expected the ambush, Jess couldn't help her surprise at how quickly the situation devolved into chaos. While she appreciated Travis' concern over her well-being, she knew she would only get in his way.

So with her emergency kit bag slung around her neck, she took to the sky and did her best to make herself scarce while keeping an eye on the situation below.

It didn't look good.

While they hadn't left with enough soldiers to create a true problem for them, the reinforcements that poured from hidden spots in the mountain put a whole new spin on the situation. They emerged and began to shoot, tranquilizers for the most part, but the less deadly missiles still proved a major issue.

Sleeping meant not fighting. Not fighting meant they got captured. And with her clan's folk out of commission, or close to, some of those firing turned their attention to the sky.

Remaining aloft was no longer an option, not with the jerks on the ground shooting at her. In order to draw their attention, and maybe give those on the ground a chance to regain the upper paw, she pretended as if she was hit, uttering a loud cry.

Thing was, her cry stopped the potshots but sent a certain grizzly on a wild rampage to rescue her.

Adorable, yet useless.

She wasn't quite certain what Travis meant to accomplish. While she did purposely weave and wobble down the air currents, it wasn't as if his bear could safely catch her unless he planned to use his body as a cushion.

A pin cushion.

With her aerial view she couldn't help but see the tranquilizing darts that peppered him. If ever there was a time for a bear to not hibernate, it was now; however, poor Travis couldn't help himself. Drugged, he couldn't keep his feet, let alone his balance. He toppled over the edge of a small cliff and slid down a rock incline.

She did a mental wince and dove a bit lower to check on him. Splayed out on a pile of small stones and hard dirt, he appeared none the worse for wear; no pooling blood evident, his chest rose and fell evenly. For the moment, he seemed safe enough. However, the same couldn't be said for the rest of their group judging by the roaring and screaming echoing from the other side of the hill.

Flapping her wings, creating her own current to soar, she popped over the edge, no higher, lest she make a tempting target. She landed on the surface of a pockmarked boulder, a perfect perch aloft where she could view the unfolding events.

Bleak.

Whilst she checked on Travis, even more men arrived for the wrong side. Frederick among them.

You treacherous bastard.

If she needed further proof of his perfidy, she now had it. No doubt remained now. The raven had shown his true colors, or color. Black, like his reputation, his heart, and, soon, the color of his blood when she spilled it and let the hungry sands of this place soak it up.

Would she feel guilty about taking his life given all the rules and morals he'd broken? Maybe a touch for the man she once knew who changed so much. Jess understood war could forge a person's beliefs, not always for the better because of the exposure to atrocities, but how could someone who'd always seemed honorable and, if not perfect, at least decent at the core when it came to people, have changed into a traitor both to his wife and his kind?

And for what? What exactly did he fight for?

That proved most baffling of all.

While these thoughts flitted through her mind, fluttering questions and feelings that spun in a vortex she wished she could bottle, she tried to see a way she could help.

How? I'm not a solider. She didn't have a gun or, really, much skill to use one if she did.

Not that one lone gun would have helped. Surrounded and felled by tranquilizers, her clansmen collapsed while Layla hung limp over someone's shoulder.

The good news, they weren't killing them. The bad, they were taking them who knew where for who knew what. And the worse news, she heard shouts of "We're missing a pair. The other bear and the doctor."

Time to duck—or should she say hawk—out of sight.

The sun projected from her back, so while her perch provided a great view, unless one of the men below wanted to blind himself staring toward the sun, they probably couldn't see her. But she wouldn't assume. *Because you know what happens then, they'll make an ass out of me.*

Never had she felt so useless. All her skills and knowledge wasted in this situation.

How can I help?

She needed to call for aid. Yay for the phone still in the bag hanging around her neck. But before she dialed for help, she needed to see if she could aid the only other person not yet captured. A certain sleeping bear who would prove way too easy to capture if anyone came across him.

Which could happen soon given the yells and sounds of men climbing the hilly ridge over which Travis had toppled. She had to move. No more wasting time.

She pivoted and toed across the rocky peak until she hit the edge of the incline Travis had rolled down, and then she shifted shapes for better traction and balance, the bag still strung around her neck.

It didn't contain much. A change of clothes, a canteen and power bar, plus a basic first aid kit. Her emergency sack, which she always wore around her neck when she went out. First rule of survival in Alaska and anywhere else.

Although time was precious, she took a moment to slap on a shirt and her sandals, not boots—which meant she hoped she didn't startle something with her painted red toes. A vanity she splurged on once every month.

She also drew on underpants and shorts because, with her luck, Travis would wake just as she stood over him with her stuff hanging out.

Light thoughts helped her to keep focused. No use panicking. Panicking wouldn't get her anywhere other than caught.

She couldn't allow that to happen, not with so many lives at stake. People she cared about.

I can't let them take Travis.

The big grizzly still lay where he'd landed. Snoring.

Loudly.

Good grief, the man made a lot of noise.

Especially grunts of annoyance as she tried to rouse him.

Shaking his furry shoulder had no effect. "Travis!" she hissed. "Travis. Wake up. We gotta go."

His muzzle twitched. He rolled his head and continued to blow air hard out his nose.

Realizing she could possibly get her face chewed off, but desperate, she grabbed his furry cheeks in two hands and shook while loudly whispering. "I can't have you passed out like this, Travis. We are in deep doo-doo. And our friends are in danger. We need to go, but you're too heavy for me to move." And no way in hell was she leaving him behind.

Rumble. Snort. Whistle. He slept, completely oblivious.

What to do? She needed to counter the effect of the sleeping darts; however, only time could truly do that. If only she could wake him for a few minutes, enough to at least move away from the area and find shelter so he could sleep it off.

A light bulb went off, and she could have slapped herself for her mental lapse. *I have a way to rouse him, long enough that we can maybe conceal ourselves in that split in the rock that I saw when I was flying earlier.* At the worst it was an alcove, in the best-case scenario a cave. So long as no one followed their scent trail, they'd at least be out of sight.

But first to rouse a hibernating beast, which meant she needed to jab him with a needle in the heart.

And then hope he didn't wake up roaring and biting.

Chapter Fourteen

One minute Travis was chasing butterflies because they were hiding his view of a naked Jess running through a field of flowers, and the next he was rolling to four feet, shaking his big, shaggy head and about to let out an epic roar when...

A hand slapped over his muzzle as someone hissed, "Don't you dare, or they'll hear us and find us."

Let them find me. I'll tear their limbs off.

His body practically vibrated he had so much energy to expend.

"We need to move and hide."

Hide? No hide. Wanna play.

The bear had no interest in running away from the danger. On the contrary, it craved it. But his bear could also smell the anxiety pouring off Jess.

Jess.

Safe for the moment.

Unlike the others, as she quickly related. "The others have been caught. There's too many for us to fight, and the adrenaline shot I gave you will wear off quicker than I'd like, especially given how much energy your bear form requires."

Conserve energy. He caught that part and, with a mental shove, because someone wasn't moving his hairy ass out of the driver's seat, took over his body again, letting it contort back to his man shape.

His naked man shape.

"Hey, Doc. What's up?"

Not his dick, thank god. This wasn't a really appropriate time to have dirty fantasies about Jess.

"Move." She looped her arm around his and

tugged him to follow the dry riverbed, his bare feet not just having to contend with the sharpness of stones but also the baked-in heat.

Here I thought asphalt in summer was hot.

Not!

While adrenaline coursed through his body, he noted it wasn't a natural energy. At the edge of it, pushing and shoving, was fatigue.

But he couldn't give in to it, not with Jess in danger. A danger that peaked when he heard a hollered, "There they are! Down in the ravine."

Spotted, but not caught.

Travis took the lead, increasing his speed, his hand dropping to lace his fingers with hers. Jess breathed in and out evenly alongside him, her slender shape fit and light, a characteristic of avian species. Or so he'd learned. He knew a lot about the different castes of shifters, all part of his fount of knowledge when it came to learning, and defending himself.

He also thought the facts he discovered were cool. He just never told anyone about his fetish for study. He didn't want to see it used against his man card. He still wasn't sure how the whole man club worked, if it graded a guy on a point system or not. Did certain actions result in a deduction of points?

And his mind was wandering.

Probably not a good idea, especially since—

Zing. The bullet hit the rock just ahead of them, and shards of stone spattered, narrowly missing them both.

"What the fuck! They're shooting at us. What happened to let's not kill them, and those fluffy red darts?"

"I think they've reconsidered and classed us as expendable in the grand scheme of things."

"Yeah, I don't think I like your assessment."

He hip checked her sideways, a quick arm around her upper body preventing her from bruising against the rock they hit. But a scraped arm on him was better than a hole from the bullet that narrowly missed them.

Thank you, Star Wars. Perhaps he didn't have a Jedi power, but Travis had spent enough time meditating—while in his bed or the hospital after some injury—to learn how to open his senses and truly have a sixth sense for the world around him. Especially danger.

"Duck!"

She obeyed without question, and the next shot whistled harmless overhead. However, their luck wouldn't hold forever. Not with the number of enemy firing on them.

"We're sitting ducks out here." Which was a comparison that made a certain grizzly bear chuff in his head.

"There's an opening in the cliff over there."

"A cave?" Better than sitting out in the open, but also a tomb if caught in there.

Options grew limited though, as more and more bullets hit the rocks. A few of the blasted shards caught them, stinging cuts along exposed skin, of which he bore plenty. His shoulder, which had gotten hit by a bullet earlier, didn't sting, not yet, but oozed sluggishly.

I might have been better off wearing my fur.

Except his wide ass would have never fit through the slit in the rock that Jess skimmed into. Latched still to his hand, she yanked at him.

For a moment, he didn't budge. The hole was small. Just enough for him to squeeze in. But then what? Wait for those attacking to get close enough and shoot them like fish in a barrel?

I'd prefer to go out fighting.

About to pry her fingers loose, a strange rumble made him pause. An ominous tinkle of rock and sand sprinkled his head. He peeked upward in time to note the wild gunshot that hit an overhang of rock.

When he'd left Alaska to come here, if someone would have said watch out for an avalanche, he would have laughed. Out here, in a land of sun, sand, and rock? As if.

However, as he noted the cliff side atop him literally shear off and begin tumbling down, he couldn't help but think, *Holy fuck, betcha that hurts more than snow.*

It also curtailed his options.

Actually it really left only one. He threw himself into the crack, with a yelled, "Move. Avalanche."

"I hate this place," Jess grumbled, but miracle of the day, she could slide farther in, and a good thing, too, because the light extinguished as tons of debris came bearing down the cliff.

The lack of light sucked, but not as much as the dust that poured into their cramped space.

Travis hacked a dirtball that sucked the moisture from his mouth. Jess emitted a smaller girly sound that he'd mock later.

Later because, dammit, he wasn't going to let them die, not here, in a mountain, in the dark, and with him naked but not buried inside the woman he loved.

I won't die before I make her mine.

Despite the dust-filled air, Jess' breathing quickened, and he could practically smell the panic rolling off her.

"What's wrong?"

Her admission, made in a tiny voice so unlike her usual confident one, "I don't like small places."

"It's not small," he soothed. "Not if it can fit my big shoulders."

"And your ego," she replied with a giggle that was borderline hysterical.

"Can you go farther?" he queried. Because despite

the fact that the mountain no longer shook and nothing seemed determined to bury them alive, it didn't mean they shouldn't look for a way out. Jess wasn't the only one not crazy about their small rocky space.

"I think we can keep going. I can't really tell." She moved slowly, taking measured steps, but to his relief, the slit they'd found extended into the mountain, and the air, while stale, didn't choke them.

He couldn't have said how long they traveled thus, nor did he want to recall the terrible anxiety that embraced him as the tight walls brushed against his wide shoulders. But he couldn't give in to panic, not when Jess clutched at him and looked to him for reassurance.

It could have been hours, or minutes, but eventually the space widened, and while slow due to a lack of light, Jess kept moving, onward, somewhere, hopefully to a room with a bed.

Travis yawned. "Can we stop for a nap?"

"Oh no you don't," Jess said, squeezing his fingers. "You can't go to sleep yet."

"But I'm tired." Surely that plaintive note didn't come from him?

"We need to keep moving, as far as we can just in case the tunnel behind us caves in because of the land slide."

"Can't I have a little rest?" His jaw cracked at the wideness of his next battle with the sudden encroaching fatigue. His adrenaline had peaked, and he was now crashing.

"I think I feel an air current from up ahead. Looks like we might get lucky and have a way out."

"You know bears need a lot of sleep," he confided, his steps slowing further.

"Maybe when we get out of this, you and I can find a bed and you can show me."

"You mean share a bed?" That perked him up for

a moment, and he shoved at the sluggishness.

"If that is what it takes to motivate you. Then yes. A bed with me. And you."

"Naked." He didn't ask. He stated.

"You are such a man."

"Yup." And proud of it. No point in sugarcoating it. He also made sure he got her to say it. "You. Me. Bed. Naked."

A rueful chuckle left her. "If we survive this, then yes, anything you want. Just keep moving for me. I think I see a sliver of daylight ahead."

Indeed, through his shrinking eyesight—damned eyelids getting so heavy—he spotted the bright slash.

One step. Slide to the next. Stumble. Knee to the ground.

A voice trying to penetrate through the white noise roaring in his ears. Eyesight blurring. Torso wavering. Falling, falling...

Follow the rabbit, Jessica Rabbit. Rawr!

Chapter Fifteen

Poor Travis lost the battle with consciousness and plummeted in slow motion toward the rough floor. She just managed to drop to her knees and slap her bag down before his face hit the somewhat gentler canvas. To those who might have criticized her for not trying to catch him? She wasn't an idiot.

Petite-framed women should never try to stop an unconscious giant of a man from falling where he wanted. Just like lumberjacks didn't sit in front of toppling trees. She preferred not to die crushed by his weight.

Although his weight pressing against her while conscious—and naked? Totally different thing.

A totally pleasurable thing and pretty much a given if they survived since Travis had extracted a promise to spend a night with her in bed, sans clothing. *Oh sweet heaven.*

But first they needed to make it out of this dire situation alive.

I need a plan. First item on her list, she needed to check where that glimpse of daylight led, hopefully not into enemy hands. Fingers crossed, she really hoped they could use whatever exit she found to escape this mountain.

Once she saw where the crack led, she needed to call for help, which, given Travis had crushed her bag, and the phone was somewhere in it, might have to wait.

As she left him behind, happily snoring, she followed the weaving tunnel a few more yards. She couldn't believe their ill luck thus far on this mission but, at the same time, wondered at their good luck.

So many times they could have died in just the

last hour, and yet, against the odds, they'd survived. Together.

A sign perhaps? She kept looking for reasons to shoo Travis away, and yet fate kept tossing them together.

Even better, when together, things kind of worked out for them. Even the landslide, which some might have considered the last straw, held a silver lining. It halted all attempts at pursuit, led to their evading capture, and given the violence of it, those chasing them probably thought them dead, which they could use to their advantage. How, she didn't know, but she'd worry about that once she discovered where the hole illuminating the ragged tunnel led.

Their uncanny luck held. As she neared the crevice, her nose twitched, and she frowned. *Is that foliage I smell?* Rare for this area, unless there was a water source.

Pausing just inside the opening out, she listened and scented as best she could. Nothing untoward tickled her gut. Poking her head slowly, she surveyed the scene.

Am I passed out in the desert somewhere, hallucinating?

Surely she'd suffered some kind of trauma because no way did she gaze upon an actual oasis amidst the rocky range they hid in.

She pinched herself. Closed her eyes, counted to ten, and opened them again.

Nothing before her changed.

Waving fronds, green and lush, a pond of water, not big, no more than eight or ten feet across and rock walls surrounding it all. A little pocket of paradise for a dusty, parched, suddenly blinking-back-tears hawk.

At least they wouldn't die trapped in a mountain.

We might survive.

But her friends might not. She doubted they'd awoken in a virtual paradise.

No time to delay. She needed to get Travis moving, and she needed to call for help. She needed a bunch of things that wouldn't get done if she spent all her time mooning over shit like her feelings for Travis, her disbelief at everything that befell her, and how pretty this spot was.

Time to shove feelings to the side and get the job done. She'd had lots of practice over the years. At least now she could put it to use.

Before descending to the tempting oasis, she returned to Travis. Passed out cold, he snored, a reassuringly, steady sound. While he did use her bag as a pillow, she still managed to snag the canteen from a side pocket, as well as slip her hand into her carryall. By jostling his head a bit, she wrapped her fingers around the phone.

She prayed as she pulled it out that it survived the abuse it went through in the last while. Kyle had outfitted them well, the sturdy case protecting her cell from the impact of a comatose bear landing on it.

It was then she noted the exit wound in his back, a small hole, with ragged edges, the blood drying. She'd have to clean it and bind it. Rummaging in her bag, she managed to snag an antiseptic wipe still in its packet, but the gauze was wedged tight under his weight. And who knew where her tiny sewing set had gotten to.

Dabbing at his wound, she did her best to squint in the meager illumination and assess the damage. By all indications, it was already healing. The bleeding had stopped, and it showed no signs of inflammation, yet. Further perusal would have to wait until she had better light and access to the entry point, neither of which would happen until Travis woke and moved his sweet, naked ass outside.

Speaking of outside, she should take care of other pressing items while she could. Canteen and phone in hand, she headed back for the water source, her pace quickening as she realized she was losing light and fast.

Good in some respects because it would make any attempts to search for them difficult, but bad as well because she had to get water and place a phone call before heading back to Travis, hopefully without getting lost in the dark.

Dropping to her knees by the pond, she first opened the canteen and drank deeply, the last few tepid mouthfuls removing the dust from her tongue. Receptacle empty, she leaned out and dipped it in the water, the rising bubbles her sign to watch. When the bubbles stopped, she immediately screwed it tight and tucked it under one arm. She really should have boiled it first, but given she didn't have a pot and didn't want to start a fire for fear of drawing the wrong kind of attention, she had to hope her shifter resistance to microbes would protect her.

Strolling back to the cave, she withdrew the phone from her pocket and tapped it to wake it. The signal wasn't great.

As a matter of fact it sucked, the mocking bar waving in and out.

Shit. She cursed as she eyed the rocky walls that loomed around and, in some cases, partially over the courtyard style space.

I need to get higher and hope I get a better bead on a signal.

But she'd do so from the rocky wall where the cave was because it sported a ledge about a dozen feet up, perfect for perching.

In this tight space, shifting to fly out might prove tricky. Her wings needed room to fan, room sadly lacking here.

Leaving the canteen just within the crevice, she stuffed the phone down her shorts and began to rock climb, something she had little experience with given she usually flew to whatever mountaintops she wanted to visit.

The tips of her fingers gripped the rough rock, abrading her gloveless fingertips. Her sandals couldn't get purchase, so she toed them off, letting her bare feet curl around the protrusions that provided foot holds.

Nimbly, and thanking the fact she kept her upper body toned, she climbed the wall until she reached the slight ledge. Sitting on it, legs dangling, she yanked out the phone and peered at its display.

One weak bar. Not much, but at least it didn't disappear on her.

Hopefully it would do. Who to call? Reid? Kyle? The military so she could rat out the sarge and his traitor team?

She vetoed the last. This was clan business. Shifter stuff. Outsiders, in this case humans, did not belong. Nor would they understand what had to be done.

Given the direness, she first called her alpha. The phone rang, two rings, three, a fourth, and she was about to hang up when it was answered with a staticky, "Who is this?"

She almost closed her eyes and sighed in relief hearing Reid's voice. Stupid really because he was thousands of miles away. But, knowing the domineering Kodiak, if there was a way to get them out of this mess, he'd move mountains and oceans to do it. "It's me, Jess."

"Jess? Where are you? What's happened? I can't r—"—a burst of white noise drowned his word—"on their phone."

She guessed at his question and did her best to reply concisely before they lost contact. "We're in the mountains. A few hours from base camp. We were betrayed. All but me and Travis were taken prisoner."

"Fuck!" No amount of static could muffle his exclamation. Reid wasn't one to couch his words.

"We need help. I don't know what to do." Which

galled. "I don't know where they were taken, but as soon as Travis wakes, we'll see if we can find a trail."

"No!" Reid barked the word. "Stay wh—"—squealing and popping erased the next bit—"get to—"

The phone died just as the last sliver of sunlight dipped below the rocky peak. It plunged her in shadow, enough that the lit electronic display and missing signal bar mocked her.

"No. No. No!" She chanted the word, yet no matter how much she waved the phone around, cursed at it, or shook it, she couldn't get it to cooperate.

She'd managed one phone call, barely, and now had to hope it was enough, but she wasn't an idiot.

What could her alpha do from Kodiak Point? No one could get here in time. No one would come to save them. She and Travis were on their own.

Actually, given he slept, the copious amount of drugs making him useless, she was alone.

In the dark.

So was it any wonder she screamed when a voice said, "What's up, Doc?"

Chapter Sixteen

Startling the woman he adored while she was perched on a sliver of rock overhead probably wasn't the brightest thing Travis had ever done. The result, however, where he caught her as she tumbled from said perch, right into his arms? Awesome.

Her bright eyes, barely discernible in the encroaching darkness, regarded him with a mix of annoyance and relief.

"You're awake."

"I am. And good thing, too, or you might have gone splat."

"I was perfectly fine until you startled me."

"Just wondering what you were doing and letting you know I was awake."

"I think you've made that clear. Would you mind putting me down now?"

He hugged her closer instead. "But I like you where you are." Where she belonged.

"Where we are is in danger and on our own."

Oh yeah. For a moment, in his pleasure at holding her, he'd kind of forgotten the whole ambush, avalanche, lives-in-danger thing.

She quickly brought him up to speed, and by the end of it all, he had only one thing to say. "Bummer."

"Bummer? That's it?"

He shrugged as he carried her down to the water, only setting her down—reluctantly—so he could lean over and cup some of the tepid liquid to drink. "What else should I say?"

"How about let's go after them? Or, come on, Jess, let's climb out and go for help?"

"One. Not only do we have no idea where they've gone, they had vehicles. No scent trail means we can't follow. Add in the fact we've got no wheels or anything remotely capable of traveling any distance fast means we have no chance in hell at catching them. Two, it is pitch-black. While I am a great climber, and a known daredevil, even I know it's a huge risk to attempt to climb out of here in unknown territory at night. We have no idea what to expect when we reach the top, and no way of seeing it." Wisdom, from him? Damn straight. Rock climbing in the dark often resulted in broken arms or concussions. Seeing as how she handled his medical file, she should trust his judgment in this.

But his doc had more of a daredevil streak than he gave her credit for. "Maybe you can't get out, but I bet I could climb high enough that, if I transformed, I'd get enough space and height to launch myself. Get us an aerial view."

"Or get shot down because they've got night vision goggles and high-powered rifles." Him, the voice of reason? Surely the sands in this hot land would freeze.

"Since when are you the rational one?" She stood over him, hands on her hips, frowning.

Rolling onto his back, hands pillowing his head, he shot her a grin. "Just because I get hurt a lot doesn't mean I don't know how to use my head. Unlike Kyle and Boris, I like to think mine is more useful than as just a hat rack." Speaking of racks, he still couldn't believe his buds hadn't appreciated the novelty antlered coat rack he got them each last year for Christmas.

"Why don't you seem worried? I mean we're stuck in a strange land, betrayed by our own side, our friends captured, with no idea how we're going to get out of here…"

He reached up and grabbed at her hand, tugging her until she sat beside him. "I'm worried. I'm just not giving in to it. Bad stuff happens." Like dads not coming home when they were supposed to. "You got to deal with it. Look past the negative parts."

"Past it to what?"

"Focus on something else."

"Such as?"

For one, the fact they were alone, for the first time, in a dangerous, and yet in a sense idyllic, paradise. "We're stuck here for the night. You. Me. And the stars." Which glittered overhead in a jeweled display that, while different from home, also provided a comfortable measure of familiarity.

"What are you suggesting?"

She would make him spell it out. "It's getting cold. I have no clothes, and neither of us thought to bring a blanket. However, if there's one thing we've both learned, being from Alaska, is how to stay warm. We're going to have to *snuggle*." And yes, his lips curved in a teasing grin.

"Travis! Now is not the time for...um...snuggling."

Nice to know she grasped his innuendo, but it sucked she rejected the idea. Perhaps with a little persuasion... "Not the time or is it? Think of it. We have no idea what tomorrow might bring. Hell, we can't even predict the next hour. I, for one, don't want to regret or wonder what could have been."

"I don't know what you mean."

"Don't lie to me. Not now. Not after what we've gone through." The darkness and the situation gave him the courage to say the words he'd held tight to his chest the past few years. "I care for you, Jess. Actually, that's not true, I love you."

"You can't." She whispered the words, but she forgot to hide the longing.

"Why not? And don't tell me because you're

mated. We both know Frederick isn't your mate. You might have exchanged vows once upon a time and meant them, but it's clear to anyone with eyes in their head that whatever bond you thought existed is gone."

"Even if you're right, and I'm not mated, you can't love me."

"Why not? I know so much about you."

"Been stalking me, have you?"

He couldn't help but chuckle. "Not quite, but I have been watching." As if he could help himself. "Every time I saw you at the medical center, I soaked in as much of you as I could. How you like to tuck your hair behind your ear when you're thinking. The fact you chew on a pen when you're puzzling something out. The way your tongue peeks between your lips when you're threading a needle."

"It does not."

"Does too, just the wee tip, and it is freaking adorable." Not to mention cock hardening because, each time, he couldn't help but picture that tongue put to better use.

"So you know my habits. How can you call that love?"

"Because I've gotten to know you. How you're selfless when it comes to others, always ready to drop everything, or wake up in the middle of the night, if someone says they need you."

"And by someone, you mean you."

"Not just me. Anyone. You care about others. You try to keep idiots like me from engaging in foolish stunts."

"To no avail."

"But at least you try. You also have a wicked sense of humor."

"I would have labeled it sarcasm."

"Whatever you want to call it, it makes me laugh.

You make me smile. You make me feel all kinds of things. Good things. It's why I fell in love with you and want you in my life."

"You haven't fully thought this through. Even if Freddie's not my mate, you do realize I'm a few years older than you."

A rumble vibrated his upper body. "Mmm. I know it. Totally sexy."

"Not so sexy is my fear of your mother."

"Which again only highlights how smart you are. Everyone's a little scared of Ma."

"I highly doubt your mother would like you getting involved with me. I'm sure she'd prefer some cute little malleable creature that would be content to stay at home and bake cookies while caring for cubs."

Yeah, his ma probably would. It didn't change how he felt. "Ask me if I care. I love my mother, but when it comes to my future, my mate, the woman I intend to spend my life with, it's my choice. And I choose you."

The way her eyes widened, he knew his words had an impact. A positive one.

To forestall any more excuses on her part, he sealed his declaration with a kiss, a kiss that ignited an inferno between them.

It seemed all his reluctant hawk needed was reassurance and touch. And he was more than willing to provide both.

Around her slim upper body, he wrapped his arms, holding a frame that trembled slightly, not in fear, but need, a need for closeness.

He maneuvered her so she sat on his lap, the hardness of his erection pressing against her bottom. How he hated the layer of clothing she wore that separated their flesh. Then again, he'd probably embarrass himself in eagerness if not for the fabric barrier. His desire for her ran deep.

Fingers threaded through her curls, he angled her head to give him deeper access to her mouth, his tongue plundering the wet recess, dueling and sliding.

She was not a passive participant in the embrace. Her hands cupped his cheeks, an intimate acceptance of what they did. They then traveled, tracing the contour of his shoulders, skimming over his flesh, leaving goosebumps of awareness behind.

When his own hands finally did their own form of exploration, she didn't stop him when he tugged her shirt upwards so he might finally touch her smooth flesh.

He didn't miss her shudder or gasp as his fingers tickled across her skin, rising up her ribcage until he cupped her small, perky breasts. Utter perfection.

"I want to taste them," he admitted in a husky voice.

"What are you waiting for?" was her breathy reply.

Permission granted, he wasted no time stripping the offending garment from her, baring her upper body, which in the gloom he could barely perceive, but he didn't need to see to feel.

And feel he did. One hand in the middle of her back, he arched her so that she presented her peaked tips to him. Each, a glorious mouthful, which he sucked. His teeth nibbled the erect nubs as her hands clasped his head, and she uttered the most arousing sounds.

Gasps. Moans. A few panted yeses.

While his mouth pleasured her sensitive breasts, he used his free hand to tug at her shorts, their elasticized waistband simplifying his task. Her panties soon followed. He cupped her sex, the heat and honey physical evidence of his effect on her.

Unbidden, but obviously in the same lustful grip as him, she straddled his lap, her hot mound pressing against his cock, which lay trapped between their bodies.

Shaking with need, he released the tip of her nipple and hugged her tight to him, skin to skin. He leaned his forehead against hers and groaned, "I want you so much."

"I do too," was her soft and startling admission.

Before he could ask if she was sure, she took control of the moment. Lifting her body, her hand slipped between them and grasped his cock. Her thumb stroked over the tip, spreading the pearl of liquid there.

Another groan escaped him then a gasp as she rubbed his swollen head against her moist nether lips.

Wet. Hot. And eager for him.

Her sex invited his shaft with a heat and moistness that almost proved his undoing.

For so long he'd dreamed of this moment. Forever, he'd tried to imagine how it would feel.

The reality proved a million times better.

As she lowered herself onto his cock, her channel pulsing around him, welcoming him and squeezing him, it was all he could do to remain in control.

He held himself still, too afraid to move, too afraid this was all a dream.

But Jess feared nothing. "Don't hold back," she whispered against his lips before slamming herself down on his lap, impaling herself with the rest of him in a fell swoop.

Ohmyfuckinggod.

He couldn't help but dig his fingers into her flesh at her sudden move, desperate to not come instantly, a fight he almost lost. Surrounded by her quivering flesh, all he wanted to do was come and mark her with his seed.

He knew he wouldn't last long. Not the way she ground against him, driving him deep. Oh fuck. Pulsing around him. Damn, it felt so good.

He managed to retain enough sense to slide his

hand down to where their bodies joined. He knew he stroked her right when she cried his name. "Oh, Travis." Even better, a shudder went through her then another.

Trembling atop him, she rocked her hips while he rubbed at her clitoris, the gentle friction making her tighten, clamp down, shiver, shake.

Come…

He couldn't have muffled his bellow if he tried. Part relief, part triumph, a lot of glorious emotion. *She's all mine. My woman. My doc. My Jess. My mate. My life.*

As he held her shuddering body in the aftermath, he couldn't help but murmur in her ear, "I love you." And while she didn't whisper it back, she did hug him tight. A new beginning for them both.

Chapter Seventeen

On the shore of their little oasis, the threat of death and danger dangling over them, they made love a second time, their movements languorous and exploratory, with her lying on her back as Travis took her with deep strokes. Long, fulfilling thrusts that had her clawing at his back, and desperate.

She came again, for a blissful slice in time able to blot out the events that led them to this place and refusing to feel guilty at snatching a small moment of pleasure. Who knew if they'd ever get another chance? Who knew if they'd even survive the night?

The closeness and intimacy of the moment filled her with a yearning to never have it end. *If only the real world didn't await us. If only we could stay here, like this, together, forever.*

"I can hear you thinking," he murmured in between soft kisses to her temple.

"And what exactly do you hear?"

"You're wondering if you did the right thing."

"Actually, I don't regret what we did." Which surprised her. The expected shame and guilt of straying from her vows didn't strike.

"I'm glad to hear that. I think you deserve some happiness."

Yeah, she did. "I'm not totally unhappy with my life. I have my friends and my work."

"Neither of which keep you warm at night or provide a shoulder to lean on."

"I'm strong." Strong enough to handle everything life threw at her so far.

"Never said you weren't. Your strength is one of

the things I love about you. But being strong doesn't mean you can't occasionally rely on someone else. Someone like me. I've got pretty big shoulders you can borrow. And I've got lots of fur to keep you toasty."

"My very own grizzly bear."

"Yours for as long as you want me, which, I'll admit, I selfishly hope is a really long time."

How easily he spoke of a future. She didn't dare think so far ahead.

As if he read her mind, he said, "I can hear your brain whirring again. You're worried we might not make it out of this alive."

"Aren't you concerned?"

She felt more than saw the smile against her forehead. "Not really. I waited too long to get you in my arms. Too long to have you recognize there's something special between us. I'm not going to let anything, not even death, steal my happy future with you."

The pessimist in her warned against placing trust in his belief, she ever was the practical one. "I love your optimism, really I do, yet look at our situation. You can't stop fate if it decides it's our time."

"I disagree. I think we make our own fate. Sometimes we even have to fight it. If I have to, I'll arm wrestle that wily bastard until he gives us the happy ever after we deserve."

She couldn't help but laugh at his vehemence. "You are too much."

Shifting against her, he growled teasingly. "That's not what you thought a few minutes ago. I would have said I have just enough to satisfy."

More than enough. She was glad the dark hid her hot cheeks. "We need to get serious. What are we going to do? My phone is almost dead. No one knows where we are. Our friends are missing and—"

"Yet we will still prevail because we have each

other."

Kisses swallowed any further pessimism on her part. His incredible stamina, and her long drought when it came to intimacy, saw them joining together for a third time, the pleasure just as intense.

Pillowed against Travis, their desires sated for the moment, she knew when he slipped into sleep, his breathing slow, his body slack, but even in repose, he wouldn't let her leave his side. He kept an arm looped around her, possessive, protective, loving.

Because he loved her.

I choose you.

Long after Travis had said them, the words still rang in her head. More potent even than the words I love you, they wrapped her in a warmth she'd never thought to feel again.

Some might mock her for finding such comfort in that simple phrase. After all, wouldn't most men choose a woman over their mother? But in Travis' case, she knew how close his bond was with the woman. To know he'd rather face Betty-Sue's wrath than give her up? How couldn't she love a man who'd do anything for her?

This is how a true mate acts. This is the commitment I should expect. A love she deserved.

It was all too clear now that the depths of her emotions for Travis didn't come close to comparing the love she thought she bore Frederick. Her relationship with him was but a pale shadow in comparison.

But did true love excuse her action? *I still cheated on my husband.*

She refrained from wincing. Mated or not, there was the matter of some vows and papers filed with city hall that said she belonged to another.

Not for long. Annulling that mistake was how divorce lawyers paid for their homes and cars. If they got out of this—make that when they did, according to

Grizzly Love ~ Eve Langlais

Travis—she'd contact one, that was if Frederick didn't suffer a fatal accident beforehand.

If she gutted and buried Freddie in the desert, would she have to wait seven years for him to be declared dead before she could move on with her life with Travis? *At worst, we could live in sin.*

As night deepened, she finally allowed herself to drift off, only to awaken rudely as she was dumped to the ground.

"Wha—"

A hand slapped over her mouth. "Shh," Travis whispered in her ear. She burned to ask him why, what danger had roused him, but then she heard it, the pinging bounce of a pebble then the scrape of something sliding over rock.

Someone or something had invaded their oasis. Friend, foe, or simply a wild animal? The potent smell of the foliage and the lack of breeze masked the scent of what came. She held her breath, lest the sound pinpoint her presence. She kept her eyes closed, blind in the deep darkness yet worried about the whites of her eyes giving her away. She also hoped to heighten her auditory senses. To no avail.

She didn't hear any more untoward sounds. Saw no predator. Smelled no predator. Touched by nothing. All her senses alert, yet none of them able to identify, which made their abrupt discovery all the more shocking.

When the spotlight shone in her face, too many watts of bright illumination, all she could do keep her eyes clamped rather than suffer through a white blindness.

Rescue?

Judging by the mocking, "Well, well, well. What do we have here?" she'd say not.

Their idyllic reprieve had come to an end. And so had they.

Chapter Eighteen

Getting caught naked without a weapon in a strange land? Kind of daunting.

Getting caught naked by the husband of the woman you just had sex with? Awkward and kind of deadly.

The bright glare of light might have blinded him to who invaded their hidden valley of paradise, but the sneering tone identified the speaker.

Frederick. Talk about luck, and he wasn't referring to the bad kind. With the raven in arm's reach, maybe Travis would get a chance to make Jess into a widow.

The situation, once dire, was already looking up, even if he was currently face down.

Hello, dirt. It's been almost a day since we last met.

Of course, he didn't kiss the ground purposely. The stock of a gun applied against the back of a head—three times because he did, after all, have a hard head—would do that to a guy.

Before a vote was taken to remove his man card for allowing himself to be captured, it should be noted he could have avoided the face plant, and easily too. Had he chosen to fight, he would have donkey kicked the bastard behind him then whipped around and taken the rifle from the asshole so he could beat him with it. However, Travis held off. Common sense—such a nasty term—prevailed.

Yet what choice did Travis have? Surrounded by at least six men, all armed to the teeth, didn't exactly roar good odds.

We could take them. Glory and mayhem could be ours.

Rawr.

If he were alone, he would have fought. Heck, his bear was begging to let him go grizzly on their asses.

However, Travis didn't just have himself to think of. Jess was with him. Sweet, vulnerable, naked Jess.

Naked!

Head angled to the side, he noted her kneeling on the ground beside him. A growl rumbled through him as he noted one too many gazes straying to her girly parts. *My girly parts.*

For a moment he considered saying fuck the odds and bucking the asshole with his knee pressing against his spine as he reefed Travis' arms back to manacle them. However, another planned formed when he realized their captors weren't just going to kill them outright, even if Frederick wanted to.

"Shoot them," the raven ordered.

"Those aren't our orders," another replied. "The sarge said the master wanted them alive."

"The bear will cause trouble."

Yeah, I will. Finally, someone who took him seriously. What a shame the guy who recognized his awesomeness was on the bad guys' side and not from Kodiak Point.

A snicker sounded. "Trouble for who? He's handcuffed and not going anywhere. I think someone's a little miffed that his wife prefers getting dick from someone else. Then again, can you blame her? Buddy's fucking hung."

Travis managed to grin and uttered a "thank you" before the kick in the ribs had him gasping for breath.

Stupid steel-toed boots. Just another reason why Frederick would die. Painfully. Perhaps disemboweled. Boris spoke highly of that method.

Feigning a meekness he certainly didn't feel, Travis allowed them to haul his heavy carcass up. He bit his inner lip, lest he grin at their grumbled complaints of him weighing a ton.

His ma had fed him well over the years. Long gone were the days of him being the runt.

The urge to smile, though, was wiped when he saw Jess getting the same rough treatment. She stumbled at the force with which they propelled his delicate hawk to her feet. She received a cuff for her clumsiness.

Travis caught the fellow's eye who dared strike a lady. "I'm going to make you scream soprano for that."

"Says the dickhead handcuffed and naked."

Scoff him? Travis smiled. Widely. Wickedly. All his teeth showing.

The fellow, some kind of dog mix, blanched.

Most excellent.

"I still think we should shoot him," Frederick grumbled as he prodded Travis in the back toward a dangling rope illuminated by their spotlight.

So that was how they'd descended into the hidden valley. Travis just wished he'd heard them sooner. He could have picked them off as they descended.

Midnight snack, his bear added with a smack of its lips.

Sometimes living with a wild animal in your head took some adjusting, especially when it came to their idea of a yummy meal. No matter how many *discussions* he and his beast had about it, Travis preferred his meat cooked, or at least singed on the outside, while his bear preferred it fresh. Sometimes too fresh. Shudder.

For a moment, Travis wondered if they'd unshackle his hands and order him to climb, but it seemed they didn't trust him. Instead, the bottom end of the rope was harnessed around his body, and once Frederick gave the dangling nylon cord a tug, Travis' feet left the ground.

Lots of boring stuff happened then. In a nutshell—pecans being his favorite— Travis, Jess, and the guys who'd located them made their way off the mountain. Most of them at any rate. The one who wouldn't stop staring at Jess' naked ass suffered an unfortunate tumble down the hillside. Who knew a simple hip check would send the lightweight flying?

After that, everyone kept their distance from Travis, and a weapon was trained on him at all times.

It was nice to be respected.

Arriving after an enforced march at a parked military-style truck, Travis wondered if it was too much to hope they would get taken to where the others were held captive. Once he rejoined his friends from Kodiak Point, they could join together to escape, kick some ass, and return home.

The large military truck they boarded was the flatbed kind with an arched canvas top over the back. Wooden benches ran the length of it.

To his relief, they weren't expected to sit on the seats naked—splinters in the ass sucked to get removed. Robes were given to them, although Travis would have preferred to have his arms in the sleeves, but apparently they didn't trust him enough to let his hands loose. They just tossed the garment over his head, creating an additional layer of difficulty by covering his manacled hands.

Awesome. He did so like a challenge.

Travis found himself shoved hard onto a bench with orders to sit while Jess got the seat across from him.

The rumble of the motor proved loud, their company less than exciting, but hey, they were alive. Alive and on their way to the secret headquarters where the rest of the gang awaited.

Anything could happen.

As to those who questioned his optimism?

Fuck off. He wouldn't give up. Not as long as he had breath.

Ignoring their companions, he leaned forward and studied Jess. Pale with her eyes downcast and appearing weary, he couldn't help but ask, "Are you all right?"

The brown eyes he'd come to love met his glance. She shrugged. "If you mean am I hurt, then no. But as for all right? Given the situation, I'd say no."

"You're worried about this?" Travis made a show of glancing left to right, staring at each fellow in turn, enough that they fidgeted and shuffled their guns. He smiled and mouthed a few taunts—*I'll be killing you soon. You look tasty.* And *Can't wait to hear you scream*—before turning back to face her. "I wouldn't worry. We'll get out of this."

"While I appreciate your lying to keep me calm, I'm not an idiot. Face it, short of a miracle, we're going to die."

"Eventually, but not today, nor tomorrow, or for many decades to come. I've got plans for you, Doc."

When she didn't reply, he prodded. "Aren't you going to ask me about my plans?"

She sighed. "Okay, Mr. Ray of Bloody Sunshine, what are your plans?"

"Well, after I kill these assholes, then free us both and our friends—"

"Shouldn't you free yourself first to kill them?" she interrupted.

"And make it too easy on myself?" He feigned complete shock and was gratified to hear her laugh.

"Okay, so you're going to kill these guys"—she shot their guards an amused look—"free us and our friends, then what?"

"Well, I thought I'd let Layla and Brody get a shot at the Naga, seeing as how they've got the biggest vendetta against him."

"Just don't let Boris near him. I heard him mention to Gene that Jan gave him some tips on cooking snake over an open fire."

The cannibalistic remark saw their guards shuffling uncomfortably. Travis exacerbated it with a grin. "Pity Ma's not here. She's got a kickass recipe for snake stew."

"I'm more worried about the ones she's got for stuffing a bird," Jess muttered.

"The only stuffing you have to worry about is the grizzly kind." Corny, and his wink probably unneeded, but the blush on her cheeks totally made the snickers worth it.

Optimism aside, Travis held a smidgen of doubt. Just a bit. They were, after all, heading into unknown territory. While he preferred to assume his friends were alive, if imprisoned, he wasn't naïve enough to think that everything would turn out well. The situation was dire, but when the chance arose, he'd do his best.

Of course his best would work better if once they arrived they didn't place him in a silver cage. Worse, they didn't put Jess in with him.

But before he began to bellow about the less than adequate accommodations, he should perhaps note they arrived much too quickly at their destination. The fact no one blindfolded them or made any attempt to mask their location didn't bode well. In the movies and on television, that usually meant the hostages would end up dead.

Then again, given they'd arrived at a rocky mountain that looked like thousands of other rocky mountains—dirt, rock, more dirt, more rock—perhaps they weren't truly worried about someone escaping and leading others back to their secret hideout.

As accommodations went, he'd have to complain to management. "Hey, how come this cell only has a hole in the ground? You can't seriously expect me to use that to do my business?" he hollered after his jailor. The grizzly fellow ignored his request for a proper room and amenities, wandering away, leaving him without a word but an eloquent middle finger salute.

"See if I leave you a tip," Travis complained.

"I knew he couldn't stay out of trouble," exclaimed Boris, who resided in a cell a few doors up from his.

"Boris, how's the rack hanging?" Travis chirped, happy to see his best bud alive and well.

"And there goes another hundred bucks," Gene grumbled from another.

"Is everyone here?" Travis asked, doing his best to peek around without touching the silver-coated bars.

"Everyone but Layla. They're holding her somewhere else," Brody growled. "Boris, how much longer?"

"Longer for what?"

"If my internal clock is ticking right, then less than an hour," Boris announced. "Give or take depending on desert traffic."

Ever get the feeling you were out of the loop? "Anyone care to clue me in?"

"You'll see," was Brody's enigmatic reply. "While we wait, why not tell us what happened to you and the doc?"

As Travis and Jess—who had the cell on the other side of Gene—filled them in—minus certain intimate details—he got the story of their own capture which was, admittedly, less exciting.

They got tranquilized and awoke in their cells. They'd yet to see the scales of their captor, although the master sergeant had apparently paid a visit to taunt them.

"I still can't believe he turned traitor like that," Gene muttered.

"Says the guy who had a vendetta against us there for a while."

"Yeah, but I never actually caused permanent

harm. Just fucked with you, mostly. What he did, leading his own men into traps and having them killed?" Travis could picture the big polar shaking his head. "That's just fucking wrong."

"He'll pay for it," Boris stated.

And Travis seconded it. "We will kick his ass."

"As soon as we get out of these fucking cages. Which is in..." Brody paused.

"Less than half an hour. Give or take."

Half an hour?

But I want to play now. A grizzly bear whining, even if in his head, wasn't pretty.

"Do we have to wait?" Travis itched to get going. The quicker they wrapped things up here, the faster he and the doc could get busy doing more pleasurable things. Naked things.

Rawr.

"Unless you have a way to bust out of these cages, which I might add are reinforced steel with a silver coating, then yeah, we have to wait."

"Is that all?"

"Is that all?" Boris snorted. "Says the cub whose hands are still tethered under his robe. At least I hope that's why they're hidden. You better not be doing anything funky under there."

"Funky? It's called masturbating."

Boris groaned. "Don't use that word. You know I hate that word. Real men say whacking off."

"Beat the meat."

"Choke the chicken." That one came from Jess, who joined the game with a snicker.

"Spank the monkey."

"Jacking off."

"Strangle the one-eyed snake."

"Buck the slobbering donkey."

Silence met Travis' contribution.

"What? It's a valid expression," he defended.

"That's just gross," Gene replied. "And how did we get so off topic?"

"Because you're guys, and everything always comes back to sex," was Jess' dry retort.

"Well, for your information, while my hands are busy under this robe, it isn't because I'm self-pleasuring. Just getting rid of some unwanted jewelry."

With some straining, contorting, and a bit of scraped skin, Travis shed the handcuffs and tossed them—with a triumphant grin of course—through the bars so they clanged on the floor.

"How the fuck did you do that?" Boris exclaimed. "That's not something I taught you."

A roll of his shoulders probably wasn't seen by his buds, but they could hear the nonchalance in Travis' tone as he admitted, "You don't get tied up as much as I do over the years and not learn a few escape tricks." He also spent weeks one summer studying the magician greats, especially their tricks on how to escape handcuffs and straitjackets. He'd picked up some cool tricks on the way. "When they placed the cuffs on me, I made sure to thicken my wrists."

"You pulled on your shifting ability?" Brody inquired, peering through his bars, yet careful not to touch the silver coating.

"More or less. It's something I've practiced. I can't do it for long, but when it comes to cuffs, you only need to hold it for as long as they're clamping them on. This left them looser than recommended. Then it's just a matter of contorting the hand"—also known as dislocating his thumb which he'd done numerous times over the years, mostly accidentally—"and slipping free."

"Hot damn. Maybe I won't lose that hundred bucks after all," Gene said with a laugh. "I told you that you all don't give the cub enough credit."

Coming from the deadly polar bear, that was high praise indeed. Travis swelled in pride.

"Free hands doesn't open cell doors," Boris argued.

"He's right," Brody seconded. "Having spent months—"

"Make that well over a year," Gene amended.

"—as a prisoner, I can attest to their solidity."

"Who said anything about busting out?" Travis snorted. "You know, not everything is about violence and brute strength."

Okay, so that might have been a tad funny. The laughter soon stopped once Brody exclaimed, "What the fuck?"

Ignoring the outburst, Travis concentrated on calling forth a single claw and sliced a line down his left arm.

"What the hell are you doing?" Brody snapped. "Now is not the time to start self-mutilation."

"You might not know this," Travis said as sweat beaded on his forehead and blood pooled from the cut, "but my dad, when he served in the army, was a bit of a badass spy."

"And this is pertinent how?" Brody asked.

But Gene already guessed judging by his guffaw. "Holy fuck. The cub's going to get us out of these cells."

Indeed he was. From the gash in his arm, Travis withdrew a lock pick and held it up so those craning could see.

Jess gasped. "You had that buried in your arm? Are you insane?"

"Not according to my therapist, although she does think I might have mommy issues."

"Ya think?" Snorted by Boris.

Tool freed, Travis went to work on the lock for the cell, pleased he'd managed to shock them all.

In that moment, he felt perversely close to his dead father. While his dad might not have lived long enough to truly impart all his wisdom onto his son, Travis never forgot that one lesson, taught to a young boy on his father's knee. Years later, stuck in a prison cell, the one piece of advice he'd learned from his father would save them all.

"Son, as shifters, we have many great abilities."

"Like eating the bad guys," wee little Travis said as he munched on a home-baked cookie.

"Yes, we can eat the enemy and maul them something good. But the fact we can turn grizzly isn't always the most important thing we can do. At least not in my line of work. We're strong, Trav. Tough. We can handle pain. We heal quickly. We do what needs to be done, no matter what. These are things the enemy, especially human enemies, either don't know or tend to forget. You can use that to your advantage."

That advantage being burying a lock pick in his arm and letting flesh heal over it, the dull ache soon forgotten, the entry wound but a thin, faded scar. Unnoticeable, yet always close at hand. When he set off the metal detector at the airport, he claimed a pin in his arm. Not his fault they assumed a surgical one.

This trick would allow him to save their asses and rescue the woman he loved.

Click.

The door to his cage swung open.

Boris whistled. "Boy, remind me to buy you a beer when we get back to civilization."

"Make that a pitcher. That is the most fucked-up, yet awesome, thing I've seen."

"And we've seen lots of shit," Gene added.

In no time at all, the cages were open.

Much as he wanted to let Jess out first, Travis went for the guys instead, knowing if trouble arrived they were better equipped to handle it.

160

Freed, Boris took one end of the room, with its single door, while Gene covered the other.

Brody rifled the few crates stored in a corner, looking for clothes Travis hoped. Mounting a rescue was well and good, but he'd rather not confront the enemy with his man parts dangling. He could have donned the robe again; however, it chafed his skin. *Someone forgot to use fabric softener.*

Last freed, and yet she didn't complain. Jess threw herself at him for a hug, which surprised and pleased him. At least she wasn't hiding their change in status from everyone.

As she gave him a squeeze, she whispered, "You're nuts."

"What about my nuts? They're still intact in case you're worried. Although feel free to check them later for injury."

She sighed. "What am I doing to do with you and your mouth?"

No way could he have stopped his laughter if he tried. "Oh, you did not just say that. I can think of lots of things we can *do*, lots of them with my mouth."

"Travis!" Funny how people could achieve a certain pitch when saying his name. Of course, when Jess did, all blushed and flushed, it was the hottest thing ever.

"If you two are done making me want to gouge out my own eyes," Gene grumbled, "then can we get this fucking show on the road. Bear boy here gave us a head start on our timeframe. I say we use it and sock it to as many assholes as we can."

"Eager to get back to Vicky?"

"Damned straight I am. My clumsy Pima needs me." Said with pride.

Just don't comment on it. Travis learned that not long after Gene's arrival in Kodiak Point. But he didn't mind those few days of eating through a straw because, while his jaw healed, he got to spend time with Jess at the medical clinic.

"So given we're changing the plan, do we opt for stealth or balls-out attack?" Brody asked.

As if there was any question.

Guess I won't need clothes after all.

Chapter Nineteen

The excitement exuded by a bunch of over-testosteroned males, jacked up on adrenaline, proved contagious to even the usually overly cautious Jess. *They're not the only ones in the mood to kick some ass.* She also had a score to settle. *Watch out, Freddie, because I am coming for you.*

While Travis, Gene, and Brody shifted into their deadly animals—a grizzly, polar bear and timer wolf, *who all walk into a dungeon and ensure no one leaves alive*—Jess and Boris—whose moose shape did better in open spaces—grabbed what they could for a weapon.

Having watched *The Walking Dead*, Jess was quite pleased with her choice of a crowbar, which she located in a crate along with some other discarded tools. The shears at the bottom did tempt—she knew someone who could use a eunuch cut; however, she wanted to kill, not maim, her treacherous husband.

Eschewing the tools, Boris opted for a board that he tore free from the crate. The rusty nails hanging out of the end of it made her mind wander for a moment—*when I get back I should check on our tetanus stock for the non-shifters in our community.*

When I get back?

It surprised her to note that her earlier pessimism seemed to have dissipated. Sure, some of it had to do with the fact that they'd rejoined the others, safety in numbers and all. Yet more of her optimism came from her growing trust in Travis. At times he might make inappropriate jokes, and get hurt a lot, but there was a smart guy under all the clowning around. A smart, wily, and sexy guy. *A guy's who is mine.*

Or would be once she hunted down dear Freddie

and made herself a widow.

Exiting their prison, they came across their first adversary, a human armed with a gun and a cell phone, head bent over the screen, the tinny speaker playing a ditty she recognized. The gaming fellow barely had time to look up and mutter "shit" before Brody lunged, taking him out. There was one Candy Crush addict who would never see what new hair-pulling madness the obsessive app would have for him beyond level 417. *If it's any consolation, you would have gotten stuck on level 421 not long after.*

One guard down, they peeked around for another. And found nothing. One measly human was the extent of the security outside their prison, which she found totally surprising.

She said as much to Boris. "Where are all the soldiers?"

The big man glanced around, and his brow knit into an impressive frown, which ridiculously enough made her want to giggle. Why? It certainly wasn't hysteria or fear, not yet at any rate. More the fact that the scowl drew Boris' eyebrows together and she could almost hear Travis quip, "Hey, Boris, you've got a furry caterpillar inching across your face."

I've got it so bad. Even when he wore his bear and couldn't speak, she could practically predict what Travis would say. Scarier, she almost said it aloud herself. *Could you imagine Boris' face if I did?* She bit her lip so as to not giggle.

Boris gave his assessment. "Could be that most of the soldiers went back to the military camp. One or two fellows going AWOL is one thing but a whole battalion of them suddenly vanishing isn't something the higher-ups can ignore. If the Sarge wants to keep his treachery secret, he'll have to maintain a façade."

"That's good news for us then," she stated.

The big man rolled his shoulders, a shrug that

neither confirmed nor denied. "Only if I'm right."

"And if not?" she asked.

Was it her or did Boris' creepy smile and grunted, "Fun times," not prove reassuring? Even more uncanny was she could have sworn the bears and wolf grinned too. Not physically possible given their muzzles, and yet, they definitely seemed chipper as they bounded and lumbered down the rock-hewn hall.

At first she thought they wandered the honeycombed mountain aimlessly, killing the occasional idiot in their path. Idiots because they saw them coming and didn't do the smart thing and run. Then again, running wouldn't technically save them.

While Brody and Gene entertained themselves swapping kills, poor Travis grumbled at the rear. It didn't take a genius to guess her grizzly bear wanted in on the action.

As did Boris, who rearmed himself along the way with weapons he stripped from the bodies. "Are you sure you wouldn't rather have a gun?" he asked as he pulled the revolver free of the holster of their latest victim.

"Am I the only one uncomfortable with the idea of shooting bullets while inside a mountain? I mean how do we know this place is structurally sound? For all we know, just a single shot could start a chain reaction that dumps hundreds of tons of rock on top of us."

"And I thought I was the pessimist in the group," Boris stated.

"Not pessimist—"

"—practical, I know." The big man rolled his eyes. "Well, Miss Practical, you hold on to your precious crowbar. I'm sure it will come in handy against guns."

"No, but using you as a shield will," she muttered.

To her surprise, Boris didn't take offence. He laughed. "That's more like it. But really, if you're going to use anyone as a body shield, I'd go with Travis' fat, furry ass. He's wider than me. He'll provide more coverage."

Indeed her bear was big, his massive grizzly shape wide enough that there were spots she feared he wouldn't squeeze through. But he did, and he provided moral support to a woman more used to dealing with the aftermath of danger than participating in it.

Whenever her breathing grew short, or she hesitated at a particularly oppressive spot—*please don't cave in now*—he would nudge her with his nose or butt her with his head. She found lacing her fingers through his fur and aimlessly scratching him behind the ears calmed her.

He calmed her, and made her feel safe.

It seemed like hours, but was probably only fifteen minutes or so, when she realized their meandering had a purpose and direction. They weren't just aimlessly wandering.

She spoke her conclusion aloud. "We're going after Layla." Which was probably a good idea, given one, she was Jess' friend and two, having Layla on their side would totally tilt the scales of this fight in their favor.

Then again, recalling a certain movie where a giant serpent tunneled from the ground and swallowed people whole made her wonder if, perhaps, Layla's powers were best left untouched. *Or I should stop watching horror movies even if I do love Kevin Bacon.*

"Where Layla is, I'll bet we find the Naga," Boris commented.

"Which is all well and good, but how do you plan to prevent his ability to control people with his voice?"

Boris never did get a chance to answer, as a door opened and a startled soldier stepped out.

And died without a scream.

So far they'd enjoyed unbelievable luck. Jess didn't like it.

"This is too easy."

"Yup," was Boris' one-syllable reply.

Nice to know she wasn't alone in thinking it, but it did lead to another question. "Should we be expecting another ambush?" Which seemed stupid. Why enable them to escape only to attack them again?

Then again, not much of the snake's actions made sense. Why take them prisoner in the first place? Why not kill them? The bad guys held the upper hand in the ambush. As they were incapacitated, they could have easily slit their throats or worse. Yet, instead, they'd awoken in a cage. To what purpose?

As they walked, the raucous sound of men gathered came to them. It grew louder as they kept following the hallway until it sounded as if they were almost on top of it. Forget seeing anything, though. The tunnel curved just enough that they couldn't see around the bend.

Did they take the smart route and send one person ahead to scout things out?

These guys? Ha.

They apparently never learned the word cautious. With just a glance between them, Brody and Gene took off at a lope, the hallway here wide enough to accommodate them. Right behind was Boris, a gun in each hand, a happy grin on his face. And was it her, or did he mutter, "About fucking time I got some action."

Poor Travis, he let out a pitiful whine but plopped his ass beside her when she stopped moving. Self-preservation demanded she not go charging into an unknown situation. Her inertia seemed to affect poor Travis, who stayed with her as a guard.

However, he couldn't hide his misery or longing look.

"You can't tell me you want to go out there?" she asked as snarls and yells filled the air.

The look he gave her said, "Duh!"

She shook her head. "Of course you want to get in on the action. You're a man." A man she loved. A man who didn't need to prove anything and, yet, felt like he had to. Wanted to.

Jess couldn't deny him that. She wasn't his mother to try and mollycoddle him and keep him safe. She just had to trust he could take care of himself and come back to her—so she could stitch him back together and berate him for being an idiot.

"Go." She waved a hand toward the unfolding sounds of chaos. "Go and help them."

She could almost hear him say, "Are you sure? What about you?"

"I'll be fine. I'll stay at the back out of trouble. Now scoot. I think they could use a ferocious grizzly."

Baring some teeth in a true grizzly grin, Travis roared and lumbered off to battle. She followed a little more cautiously. Stepping around the bend, she slowed even further as she took in the scene. *Welcome to hell.*

It seemed they'd found the bulk of the enemy's troops and caught them while they partook of dinner.

Trestle tables boasted the remnants of a meal, and the benches lining it held men, men currently engaged in battle with a wolf and a polar bear while Boris aimed and shot those who thought to raise a weapon.

But three against almost twenty wasn't the best odds.

Travis, who had halted upon entry, swung his head from side to side as if undecided what to do.

Given her lover was a bear and couldn't utter one of his trademark smart-asseries, Jess, obviously suffering from dehydration, insanity or other channeled his spirit, and said, "Look, Travis, we're just in time for dessert. Who's in the mood for blood pudding?"

Rawr!

Apparently, he liked the comparison because he

ran into the fray, engaging the attention of a few, which relived pressure on the others.

Stay safe, she prayed, hoping their decision to attack instead of escaping and going for help wouldn't cost them any lives.

Clutching her crowbar in a sweaty hand, she hugged the wall, keeping it at her back so no one could sneak up on her. She freely admitted she wasn't a fighter, but she would defend herself if needed.

Even with so much action going on, a part of her still noted when a door at the far end of the room opened.

And look who peeked out.

Frederick.

Jess tightened her grip on her weapon. *You dirty, rotten bastard.* How she hated him. Maybe in this one instance, she could instigate injury instead of preventing it.

Given the violent battle, she expected Frederick to join his crew.

She was wrong.

Withdrawing his head, he shut the door. And it stayed shut.

What to do?

The smart, responsible thing was to stick to her wall and wait until the guys finished what they started. Then, as a group, they could go after Freddie and whoever else hid behind the door.

But what if Freddie escaped? What if, while she hesitated, the Naga got away with Layla?

Once the questions arose, Jess knew she had to see what lay beyond the portal. Another room, an escape tunnel, the entrance to hell?

As she made her way around the perimeter of the room, doing her best to keep an eye on the snarling, scratching, roaring, and even howling going on, she maintained a tight grip on her crowbar.

Whether or not she'd have the pluck to use it remained to be seen. Despite all her determination to end Freddie for his crimes against her and the clan, she wondered if she'd have the nerve. She needed to decide soon, as his distinctive scent grew stronger the closer she edged to the door.

She paused and took a deep breath.

He's in there.

Question was, should she wait for backup or go after him? Because she could tell right now he wasn't alone. The dry, musty aroma that tickled her olfactory sense, while unfamiliar, stirred her bird side.

Reptile. As in snake. As in the one they'd come for. Plus a more exotic cinnamon smell she recognized. Layla.

At least three of them in there. Two most definitely not on her side.

She cast a quick glance over her shoulder. The fight was going strong still. She could expect no help from that quarter, yet the murmur of voices, the crack of flesh hitting flesh, and a cry of pain from beyond the portal let her know she couldn't wait.

"I'm a doctor, not a hero," she muttered. Not being an action hero, though, didn't mean she could stand by and not attempt to save a life.

She placed her hand on the door handle and turned.

It didn't budge. Locked.

Well, that was unexpected.

She eyed the crowbar in her hand. Looked like it would get some use after all.

Whack.

It took three attempts to knock the handle off, and there went her element of surprise. She used her foot to nudge the door open. Given its weight, it only opened partway, not enough for her see fully inside, but enough to realize it led to another room.

Don't go in.

Common sense told her to stay where she was, but it seemed the adrenaline of battle was contagious. She took a step in, pausing inside the doorjamb, the gloom of the room and the door itself still blocking her view. She placed a hand on the door and pushed.

Dear heaven.

Transfixed by the sight before her, she barely reacted when an arm wrapped around her neck in a chokehold.

It didn't take Freddie's triumphant, "You should have stayed in your cell," to realize she'd made a grave mistake.

Her hawk flapped and kree-ed in her head. Upset at how she'd allowed herself to get trapped. *Danger.*

However, Freddie wasn't the most dangerous thing in the room.

Nor was Layla, whose slack-jawed expression and glazed eyes spoke of some pretty potent drugs.

Nope. The most dangerous thing in the room was sitting coiled on its tail, a mottled gray and green sinuous monstrosity with a misshapen rattle at the end. If it were all snake, it wouldn't have proven so morbidly fascinating, but its upper body remained human-shaped, albeit covered by a dark robe. Only yellow eyes, vivid and spiteful, glared from the holes in the head covering.

A raspy voice managed to make itself heard over the raucous sound of battle. "Welcome, Jessss."

Kind of busy with her throat being crushed by Freddie, Jess didn't reply.

The hooded head tilted as it perused her. "Thisss puny thing isss your wife?"

Jess couldn't help the shiver at hearing it speak, the hissing S jarring.

As his hold relaxed a fraction, Freddie replied, "Yup."

Having sucked in a breath at the reprieve, Jess managed to croak a retort. "Not his wife by choice. Set me free and give me a few minutes. I'll make myself a widow."

The hold around her neck tightened, as Freddie growled in her ear. "Such cocky confidence."

Gasping for air, she clawed at his arm, certain she was breathing her last, but Freddie eased after a moment.

Jess drew a few deep breaths then replied. "More like certitude. Only one of us is leaving this room alive." And she dearly hoped it was her, even if Freddie held the upper hand or, in this case, arm around her neck.

"I'm getting mighty tired of dealing with you."

"I'm beyond tired. Let's get this done."

"Yesss. Let's finish thisss. Die, ssslut."

The slithery sound rolled over Jess and left goosebumps in its wake. While hoarse and somewhat discordant, the voice possessed power. Magic. An ability to force people to do its bidding.

While not much was truly known about Nagas—their kind deemed too dangerous to live and thus hunted to the death—Jess had read about them on the flight over. According to reports, their scales were tougher than any armor. Only the sharpest of blades, and the most deadly of bullets, could hope to pierce. Their tougher than armor snake skin against claws and teeth? The best a predator with fangs and fur could hope for was to inflict some irritating scratches.

So weapons were required if you wanted any hope of incapacitating it, but even if you scored a hit, Nagas enjoyed ridiculous regenerative powers. They could regrow limbs with enough time. Heal in minutes what took other shifters hours. The only sure way to kill them was decapitation and fire.

Yet their healing power wasn't what made them so dangerous. Their voices had the ability to enchant. It was said that a Naga's voice could make you do whatever it wanted.

Kill your family and not even blink an eye.

Forget your past life and work for the serpent, causing mayhem.

It seemed farfetched, yet the evidence was all around them and back at the military camp, where dozens seemed to be under the snake's sway.

And if a Naga told you to die, why, a person's very heart could stop beating. Instant death.

Or not.

See the serpent's voice relied on some odd use of harmonics and intonation, how much Jess couldn't have said, but the hypothesis that it wasn't magic but some odd form of hypnosis was the prevailing theory about how their siren-like ability worked. Or worked on most folk.

Having done her research, Jess could have laughed—with hysterical relief—when it failed on her.

Never had Jess been so happy that she was completely and utterly tone deaf. She also lacked rhythm, but a few cocktails never stopped her from jiving on a dance floor if the right song came on.

Back to the snake, which again hissed, "Die ssslut."

A wicked smile stretched Jess' lips as, once again, the creepy voice tickled at her and gave her an urge to eat artery-hardening fast food. A slow death. But definitely not the instant one the snake expected.

Cocking her head, Jess, once again, couldn't help but channel Travis, starting to understand the appeal of a good taunt in the face of impossible odds. *I won't give this creature the satisfaction of seeing me scared.* "First off, I resent the label of slut. I hardly call me sleeping with one guy in the last couple of years slutty, not when hubby dearest has been cheating on me all this time."

Rough laughter bubbled forth from under the cloak. Laughter that was higher pitched than expected.

Jess frowned.

"I would apologize for ssstealing your husband, but he doesss fill my needsss ssso well. Don't you, my sssexy lover?" Purred in a husky tone.

Lover?

"My pleasure, bella," Freddie replied with an affection she'd not heard since he'd left to serve abroad.

Puzzle pieces clicked into place. "You're a woman?"

"Sssurprise," exclaimed the Naga.

"But why hide it?" Probably not the brightest question of the moment, but Jess found herself wanting to understand why the snake chose to hide her sex.

And like most villains who'd lost a few screws during their lifetime, the Naga explained.

"My birth land is not a place that likesss taking ordersss from a woman. And I cannot constantly compel. Even I have limitsss. But if they think I am a man, a strong man like my father wasss…" The serpent trailed off, but her meaning was clear.

"Okay, I can understand why you'd hide your gender, but what about the rest? Why are you doing this, ambushing and hypnotizing folk? Why attack us? Why subvert those poor soldiers to do your bidding? What are you hoping to accomplish?"

"Asss if you don't know. For revenge, of course."

The words, "Revenge for what?" died before getting spoken, as the Naga finally revealed herself in all her gorgeous, voluptuous splendor—and horrifying reality.

As gloved hands lifted and flung the bulky robe to the side, Jess could only gape.

Oh my god.

Hour-glass in shape, if one ignored beyond her waist there was a coiled tail, the Naga's upper body was curvy with full breasts encased in a thin tank top. Full lips with just the tips of poisonous fangs peeking, bright eyes, long, dark, lustrous hair, at least half of her was model gorgeous. The other half, though…

"What happened to you?" Jess breathed the query in a whisper, aghast at the extent of damage done to the woman. Some of it recent.

Scarred flesh, rippled, shiny in spots, creviced and horrible, marred the left half of the snake woman's body.

"You're a doctor. You tell me."

"Fire." One of nature's deadliest weapons. A bane not just to vampires but shifters too. Burn enough flesh and even their shifting ability couldn't heal cauterized skin and tissue. "But how? Who?"

A throaty laugh, tinged with madness, sent a shiver through Jess. Forget rationalizing with the woman. Even a bottle of the strongest meds wouldn't cure the psychosis that shone from her eyes.

"Who? None other than those you would call friends."

"They set you on fire?" Jess had a hard time believing the guys could be so cruel. Surely they would have killed the Naga first.

"Not intentionally. Sssee, I wasn't their target. My dear father wasss. And yet, they never thought to look further than the main tent when they poured the lamp oil everywhere and lit it. They never knew a young girl, a teenage girl, ssslept in the back. But while I did burn, they didn't kill me that day. I sssurvived. I healed. And I took my father'sss place. I learned to use my powersss. I practiced on those I could, and then when I'd amasssed the needed ssstrength, I went after those who killed my father and maimed me."

Everything led back to vengeance. Yet revenge

for wrongs didn't excuse the snake woman's behavior. "But you hurt innocents while exacting your retribution," Jess pointed out.

"Just like they hurt an innocent on their mission to kill my father."

"Two wrongs don't make a right," Jess quoted.

"But blood makesss everything feel better. It tastesss good too. Enough though. I tire of you. I asked my men to keep you alive that I might meet the ssslut who kept my lover chained. But now that I have"—the Naga flicked a forked tongue, and her lips curved in a less-than-reassuring grin—"I am in the mood for roasted fowl."

"Not today, bitch." Layla, whom Jess had counted out of the equation given her drugged appearance, lunged upward and clocked the snake woman in the face.

Damage-wise, it didn't accomplish much, but it did create a diversion, enough that when the room suddenly filled with furry bodies, and a gun-toting Boris, Frederick dragged her to the side, deeper into the shadows.

"Ssstop!" The yelled command froze the chaos in the room for a moment.

Only a moment because, despite the order, Boris raised his gun and aimed for the Naga's heart.

"I command you to ssstop," the psychotic woman hissed, anger contorting her beautiful side into something ugly, something that matched the warped soul she hid inside.

Boris smiled and pointed to his ears. Rather, at the bright yellow globs in them. Ear plugs. Which meant...

Boom.

The gun went off, and someone screamed. Jess couldn't tell who, not when Frederick shoved her to the ground, the impact bruising her knees, but of more concern was the gun pointed at her head.

What are the chances he misses at this close range?

"Move one more step, bear, and she dies." Freddie's threat had her focusing ahead of her instead of on the gun.

Much better view if one didn't mind confronting a gigantic grizzly bear with his muzzle pulled back in a snarl, big teeth gleaming.

She'd never seen anything more awesome. *He's trying to rescue me.*

What she couldn't figure out was how. As a bear, Travis could never hope to rush in and knock the gun free before Freddie fired.

Apparently, he came to the same conclusion because he halted, and changed bodies.

Witnessing a shift always held a certain level of fascination. The way fur melted back into flesh, how limbs shrank and contorted to retake human shape, and yet through the metamorphosis, one thing always remained the same. The eyes.

Travis' steady brown gaze held hers the entire time, and it was to her he kept looking—*don't worry. I'm here. You're safe*—even as he replied to Frederick's threat.

"Kill the doc and you die for sure. I'll just make sure it's more painful. And long. Really long. With lots of screaming." How a naked man with empty hands could sound so threatening she couldn't have said, but she had no doubt in her mind that Travis meant every single word.

The adorable idiot.

The threat saw the gun swivel from her temple to aim at Travis, naked and unafraid Travis, who stood boldly in front of Frederick, about fifteen feet at most, which meant no way could Freddie miss. It didn't stop her bear from smirking in challenge.

"Only a coward resorts to using a gun."

"Or the man who intends to walk away the victor by any means necessary."

"Chicken." And oh yes, Travis did cluck.

Jess could practically feel the rage simmering within Freddie. "Name calling. How juvenile. But I'm going to ignore it and give you one last chance. Leave now, bear, or you will die."

"Funny. I was about to say the same thing to you. Except mine was more along the lines of I'll give you a twenty-second head start, then I'm going grizzly on your ass."

The hammer on the gun cocked back. Jess held her breath as she silently prayed for Travis to shut up and stop antagonizing her wretched husband. Although, with Freddie's attention elsewhere maybe she could—

"Don't you dare point that gun at Travis."

That voice. Jess knew that voice.

Oh my god. No way. The cavalry had arrived in the nick of time. She snickered. Things had just risen to a new level of interesting.

Chapter Twenty

Travis groaned. No. This couldn't be happening. Not now. Not ever.

But he only had to take one sniff to know his worst nightmare had come true and stood at his back.

Ma had come to the rescue. And of course had to meddle.

"Touch my baby and I will string you up by your ankles, bird. I will pluck your feathers one by one then douse you in some flour and seasoning before I deep fry you a crispy golden brown."

Peeking over his shoulder, Travis got a peek at his meddling parent—who made him crave a bucket of breaded chicken with homemade fries.

Gone was the wooden spoon she usually wielded. In its stead, his mother—dressed for a nice summer day in pink capris with numerous pockets, a flowered blouse, a satchel hung cross-wise over her chest, along with a wide brimmed hat—held a mini Uzi aimed at Frederick's head.

Her timing was great, but still… "Ma, I had this under control."

"If by under control you mean you were facing a fifty-fifty chance of survival depending on if this mangy bird's aim was any good, then, yes, I guess you did."

His pouted scowl didn't move her at all. He growled. "What are you doing here? You're supposed to be in Kodiak Point." Baking and staying out of trouble like other boys' mothers.

"When I heard my baby boy was in trouble, I had to come with Reid and the rest."

"Reid's here?" Jess interjected. Kneeling on the

floor, her hair still caught in Frederick's tight fist, her predicament distracted Travis from his mother's presence.

There was still time for him to salvage this situation and show himself a hero in Jess' eyes. A man worthy of her. "It doesn't matter why you're here. I'm a little busy so if you don't mind…" He pointedly turned his back on his mother, who harrumphed.

He ignored it, focusing his attention on Frederick. "It's over, dude. Let Jess go. Surrender nicely and maybe we won't kill you."

We, as in Travis and his ma. He highly doubted Boris and the others would prove so forgiving.

However, it seemed living a few more hours wasn't in Frederick's plans for the future. Just not for the reason any of them expected.

"Enough of this. Freddie, I want out of this marriage," Jess snapped. As she spoke, her hand darted out, fingers replaced by pointed yellow claws. She dragged them across Frederick's thigh, and immediately, a bead of blood appeared.

With a snarl of rage, Frederick flung her from him and pointed his gun at her head. "You fucking bitch. I should have killed you as you disembarked from the fucking plane. Say good—" Frederick paused, and he wobbled as blood jetted from his leg.

Hmm. Was it just him, or did Frederick seem to be bleeding an awful lot? As in puddle amounts.

"What did you do to me?" Frederick slurred as his eyes crossed and he slumped to his knees.

Wearing a smile of triumph—edged with a bit of sexy wicked—Jess rose to her feet and confronted the prick. "Just because I swore an oath to save lives doesn't mean I don't know how to take them. That teeny tiny cut? Yeah, it was to your femoral artery. I say you've got another thirty seconds before you bleed out."

"Only if I don't stop it," Frederick gasped as he plastered a hand to the gushing red tide.

Jess smirked as she lashed out with her foot and kicked his hand away. "Can't defend and hold a gun on me at the same time."

Ma, who'd sidled to Travis' side, whispered, "Remind me not to get on her bad side. That gal's got serious surgeon skills."

"I know." Travis couldn't help the edge of pride. Sure, he wasn't the one who got to tear a limb off Frederick and beat him with it. Or dangle him from a precipice, hearing him beg before dropping him on his head, but in a sense, wasn't this better? Jess deserved retribution and closure for what this prick had done to her.

Not to mention, if one ignored the messy puddle of blood, there was a certain elegance in her methods. A certain quietness too.

Frederick died without any screaming, but the incredulity on his face would linger forever.

"Until death do us part," Jess said as she rose to her feet and stood over a dead Frederick.

Or not so dead.

A hand shot out and grabbed at her ankle, throwing her off balance.

In a flash, Travis was there, stomping the offending limb, and for good measure, he wrung the bird's neck. This was one dead husband who wouldn't come back to life—or feed them for dinner.

"What a shame he didn't shift before he died," his mother lamented. "I had so many recipes I could have tried."

And on that disturbing note, they went looking for their friends.

Last Travis saw, they were confronting the horribly scarred snake lady. Boris, being a smart guy, aimed for the chest, but the Naga moved, and it hit her shoulder, causing her to utter a very shrill shriek—worse than nails on chalkboard. The second shot took her through the throat, which, given the snake woman's powers, was probably a good thing as Travis hadn't stuffed his ears with plugs before charging after Jess.

At any rate, while they'd parlayed with Frederick, the Naga had slithered off with his friends in close pursuit. They'd not gotten far, though. The crazy snake lady held them at bay, armed with a semi-automatic in a large cavern filled with parked vehicles.

Travis halted just inside the tunnel before the dangerous and psychotic woman saw them. "Jess, you and my mom stay here while I go give the boys a hand."

A dual, "not happening," made him groan. Stuck with two headstrong women in his life. Good thing he loved them—in different ways of course!

"Fine, come if you must, but stick close to me." That way, if the Naga had any kind of aim, he could use himself as a shield.

Luckily, the squealing snake woman didn't spot him. Nor did she seem capable of speech at the moment, the wound in her throat not yet healed.

It took only a short jog to dash from the tunnel to the side of a Jeep where Brody and Gene hunkered as men. Sitting cross-legged on the ground with them, Layla wore a look of concentration, which meant she worked on getting reinforcements. As for Boris, he cursed and banged his gun off a rock.

"Stupid, cheap, jammed piece of shit," he grumbled. Well, that at least explained why the Naga still lived.

"What's the plan?" Travis whispered as he dropped to his knees to join them.

"We need to set the bitch on fire," Brody stated. "But none of us have any lighters."

Trust his mother to pull a packet of matches from her slacks.

Gene grinned. "Nice. I don't suppose you got any lighter fluid in there too?"

His ma snorted. "Nope, but who needs lighter fluid or even matches when you've got a propane tank off to the Naga's left and a sharpshooter in your midst."

"But Boris' gun is—"

His mother stood, took aim with her Uzi, and, with perfect control of her recoiling weapon, fired.

Travis gaped. They might have all gaped as she calmly hit her target and shit exploded. Literally.

Lucky for them, the Jeep they hid behind protected them from most of the explosion's impact. The Naga didn't fare so well.

Given the damage to her voice, they didn't hear the monster scream, but they did see the serpentine woman undulate, the flames licking at her skin. But she wasn't done with her reign of chaos yet.

The weapon the Naga held fired, an erratic stream of bullets that didn't come anywhere close to them. However, the arcing and spitting bullets had to impact somewhere. In this case the roof of the cavern.

A trickle of dirt rained down. A few rocks followed.

As the heat and smoke thickened in the large room, a rumble shook it.

An ominous sound. Yet not as scary as the huge boulder that fell from the ceiling and crushed the hood of the Jeep they hid behind.

"Cave in." Jess breathed the word, and he didn't need to decipher her tone to read the terror in her eyes.

His hawk, a lover of wide-open spaces, didn't like tight spots, and the idea of getting buried alive absolutely terrified her.

As if he'd let that happen to her.

"Run!" Brody yelled.

While the others immediately took stock of the situation and bolted for the tunnel, Jess stood in frozen horror, eyes wide as she watched the chunks of falling stone.

"Time to go. Last one out of the mountain's a rotten egg," he quipped. Grabbing Jess by the hand, he jogged toward the tunnel where Ma and his friends went, only to stop abruptly as a bigger tremor took away their nearest option.

Travis had just enough time to duck her face against his chest before the puff of dust and debris hit them. He shut his eyes against it, and when he opened them again...

Jess said it best. "Oh my god. We can't escape. We're screwed."

Yeah, the pile of rubble blocking their way out kind of sucked.

But it didn't mean they were done yet.

Fingers still laced with hers, Travis dragged her farther into the cavern, closer to the fire and smoke that radiated heat and ash, not exactly a pleasant accompaniment to the trickling sand and stone.

It took Jess a moment to notice their new route, and when she did, she beat at his hand, panicked, fluttery hits.

"What are you doing?" she yelled. "We need to get back to the tunnel."

"The tunnel is blocked. We won't be getting out that way."

His assertion made her groan. "Maybe we could dig. Or shift a rock or two."

"No time. We have to escape now. Have a little faith, Doc. I'll get us out of here." Because Travis had a theory. The tunnel they'd entered through was too small to get the vehicles in, which meant—

Aha. Where the smoke swirled the most, he spotted, through tearing eyes, the exit. Coughing, and sputtering, he led them to it, and when Jess' step faltered, he tossed her over a shoulder and ran for the wide opening.

Even once in the wide tunnel, the fresher air flowing in a reprieve for his aching lungs, he didn't stop running, not when the ominous rumble rolled and thundered around him. The very ground under his feet shook.

He pushed harder, faster, lungs straining, eyes streaming from the grit in the air. He lunged for the open space where daylight beckoned through the fog of smoke and dust.

He exited onto a flat plain and let out a roar of triumph.

Rawr. *We made it.*

Setting Jess on her feet, he grinned and said, "Told you I'd get us—"

Boom!

The mountain behind them shook and shivered. The ground under their feet moved. But it was the second explosion, spewing debris, that proved most hazardous.

Hello concussion number ninety-nine.

Chapter Twenty-one

Cradling Travis' head in her lap, Jess knew better than to fret at the amount of blood that initially poured from the scalp wound. Those bled the worst. The lump the flying rock left on his temple also caused only a momentary pang. She knew he'd gotten bigger knocks playing football.

Yet all her medical knowledge didn't help with the anxiety knotting her stomach. Despite having escaped the mountain, they weren't out of danger yet.

Jess was out in the middle of who knew where, with an unconscious man, no vehicle, no cellphone, no supplies, nothing but herself.

The old her would have seen the situation as extremely dire. The pessimist in her would have lamented their ill luck. But it would seem her time with Travis had helped change her. She found the positive.

We weren't crushed to death.

I'm alive.

He's alive.

I love him.

I'm a widow. Good grief. I'm free.

Which means…

Things will turn out all right.

Because she wouldn't allow any other option.

With that in mind, she stroked the hair from Travis' forehead. "You brave, foolish, lovable man. What would I do without you?"

"Invest in lots of batteries?" He peeked out of one eye as he said it, and his lip curled in a grin.

She jabbed one of his bruises and made him yelp. "Can't you ever be serious?"

"Nope." No hesitation.

"Good thing for you I kind of like it."

"Only kind of?"

"Okay, maybe love it. And possibly, maybe even love you."

"No possibly about it. What's not to love?"

"The fact you probably go through ridiculous amounts of clothes because of your shenanigans."

"Yeah, but on the other hand, I'm keeping our economy working. So is it really that bad of a thing?"

She couldn't help but laugh. "How do you do this? Here we are in the middle of nowhere. Lost. Alone. With no idea of where our friends are or how they fare, and yet, I'm still happy. Happy we're alive. Happy you're with me. And despite the evidence, I even believe we'll make it out of here and get back home."

"Because we will. This is our fairy tale ending, Doc. We slayed the dragon lady. We killed the evil suitor. We went through hell and back for each other. And now it's time for our happily ever after. So plant one on me, Doc."

"Plant what?"

"A kiss of course. All princesses kiss their prince in the end."

Indeed they did.

Forget the grime coating them, and the forlorn landscape, she leaned forward and pressed her mouth to his. It wasn't a fervent, hungry embrace, but it was powerful nonetheless.

As their lips caressed and clung, she could almost hear the promise in them.

I love you. I will be with you forever. From this day forward, we are one. We are mated. We love.

How she loved. Cradling his face even as he strained upward to taste more deeply of her mouth, she felt the hunger stirring within her. The need for this man who taught her to believe in life and happiness again.

Travis dragged her down until she lay atop him, his hands cupping and palpating her ass while his tongue plunged to dance with hers.

Who knows how far things might have gone if not for the yodeled, "Travis, stop manhandling the doc. We need her services."

Before, Jess might have flung herself away from the situation and blushed or pretended to ignore what had just happened. New Jess gave his tongue one last suck and whispered, "Later."

Rawr.

Did I just hear something roar in my head?

Before she could wonder at her mental state, another voice joined Boris'.

"My baby! Oh my poor baby, covered in blood. Don't worry, Travie-teddy, Mama's here."

He shifted to a seating position with a wince.

Ignoring the approaching group, all people she recognized from Kodiak Point, all alive, Jess' expression turned to concern. "What's wrong, Travis?"

"I'm pretty sure I just heard my man card disintegrating into a zillion pieces."

She snickered. Then snorted. Then outright laughed. Laughed and laughed, even wiped a few tears as Betty-Sue threw herself on her poor Travis and dabbed at his face using a cloth she wetted from a canteen she must have pulled from her ass because, really, where the hell did the woman keep yanking supplies from? She didn't have that many pockets.

Turned out, Reid came prepared. Not only did they have vehicles stashed nearby, but they also had clothes and medical supplies and even some much-needed food. What they couldn't provide was privacy.

That embrace and instance of intimacy proved to be their last private moment until almost a day later when they were on the plane, heading back home. Given it was a late flight, most of the travelers slept, except for Travis and Jess. They were finally kind of alone, and seated together, his hand laced around hers.

"Are you thinking what I'm thinking?" he whispered.

"Probably not," she admitted because, really, who knew how her grizzly's mind worked? It was one of his better qualities. She kind of looked forward to his unexpected acts and outbursts. They made life interesting.

"Two words, Doc. Mile high."

"Are you insane?" she hissed, yet unable to stop her pulse from speeding up.

"Crazy in love. You?"

Crazy in love, too. Which was why she allowed him to lead her to the back of the plane and the tight squeeze of a bathroom. Given it was a private charter, they didn't quite have to worry about a crowd of passengers banging at the door or a stewardess, but there were challenges. Such as space.

Trust her bear to have it already figured out.

"Face the mirror," he murmured as he nuzzled her ear, his hands at her waist and already turning her.

Her reflection stared back, cheeks flushed, eyes bright, lips parted in expectation. Was that truly her?

It was. The new her. The new Jess, who would no longer live in the shadows doing her job and hoping for a brighter future.

And excitement.

With Travis around, she'd never lack for anything again, especially not pleasure.

His hands slid under her shirt, sliding up the smoothness of her stomach to cup her breasts. The brush of his thumb over her nipples turned them into tight buds. Buds that would have to wait for a suckling given their tight quarters, but in the meantime, she could enjoy the teasing pinch and roll as he took them between his thumb and fingers to play with them.

A soft sigh of enjoyment escaped her, and she leaned her head back. He took advantage, his lips caressing the exposed column of her throat as he toyed with her nipples.

But that kind of play wasn't enough for either of them. Burning with need, Jess undid her own pants and wiggled her hips so they'd slide down. She caught his expression in the mirror as she took charge of the pace.

Fierce hunger shone in his eyes. Tenderness too. And when he cupped her mound with his big hand?

Possessiveness.

His.

Finally. Someone who wanted her. Loved her.

She trembled at his touch. Wetted herself too, the sweet honey kind.

He rubbed his damp fingers against the lips of her sex, heightening her pleasure and need, shortening her breath with anticipation. Her hips rotated in time to his strokes. His finger found her clit and played with it until she thought she would go mad.

"Now, Travis. Please. I need you."

He didn't reply with a cocky remark. Instead, all serious and intent, he fumbled at the closure of his jeans until she felt the probing hot tip of his cock against her backside. He adjusted it so that it slid between her thighs, its silken length rubbing against her heated sex.

She leaned forward, hands braced on either side of the sink, projecting her buttocks, an open invitation.

He took the hint and, with his hands on her hips, angled himself so that the head of his dick poked at her nether lips. With but a simple thrust, he was in. In and stretching her gloriously.

She exhaled, and moaned in enjoyment, loving how he filled her. As for when he began to actually thrust? She panted and keened, so close to the edge.

She needed only his bold strokes to reach the pinnacle, but it was when she glanced in the mirror and caught his gaze and saw him mouth, "I love you, Doc," that she came. Came hard. Came in shuddering waves. Came and didn't come alone.

Travis joined her, the hotness of his seed marking her womb while the intimacy that joined them, the vows both spoken and thought, bound them.

We are mated. We are one.

Now and forever after.

So wouldn't you know, Travis had to be himself.

"Mated and a member of the mile high club at the same time. Rawr."

Yup, that was her lover. Good thing she didn't mind his grizzly kind of love.

Epilogue

In a little town in Alaska called Kodiak Point, where the inhabitants might wear clothes but hunt in fur by the light of the moon...

While certain members of Kodiak Point were flying home, a few stayed behind to deal with the mess the Naga left behind. With the enemy boss dead, her hold over the soldiers died too. The end result in some cases wasn't pretty. Some men immediately went AWOL, literally running off into the desert, screaming, their minds damaged by the things they'd done under her command. Others put in for counseling, their gazes haunted by the atrocities they could remember participating in and, worse, enjoying.

Then there was the Sarge, who, as it turned out, knew full well what he'd done the entire time.

"Why?" Brody asked as they cornered the rhino in the military camp. The master sergeant sat at a table in his tent, a glass of whiskey in hand, and didn't so much as flinch when they raided his space. The old man had too much pride to run from his actions.

"Why the fuck not? I spent my life giving to the military. I gave them my youth. I lost my wife in my dedication to it. And yet, despite all my years of service, they were planning to put me out to fucking pasture. Said I was getting too old. Me, too old. I'm better than most of the young'uns under me."

"So because you would have had to retire, you betrayed the soldiers under you?" Boris couldn't help his incredulity.

"Gene betrayed you, and yet I see you welcomed

him back with open arms."

"He never actively killed those who trusted him. And he's repented his acts. You though?" Brody sighed as he shook his head in sad resignation. "There is no forgiveness for what you did."

"So kill me." The ex-master sergeant held himself proud, and it didn't take a mind reader to see he expected to die. Wanted it. Wanted the glory of dying for a cause since none of the wars he fought in did him the favor of making him a hero or a martyr.

"I think dying's too good for you. You need to pay for what you've done. Starting now. You're been dishonorably discharged from the military. As such, you forfeit all your benefits, including your pension. We've also revoked your passport, and there is a customs warning should you try to enter the country. Since you love this land so much, you get to live here for the rest of your days. An outcast. A disgraced one."

With each pronouncement, the old man's face paled, and by the end, he physically flinched. "You can't do this. It's not the shifter way. You were supposed to kill me."

"Not today, Sarge."

And with that, they walked out of the tent, leaving the rhino behind to bellow. A man broken. A man alone.

But we should rewind a bit, as surely there were those who wondered how Travis' mother, along with Reid and the rest, found them in the first place? Simple. Even before Jess called, Reid and the others were on their way, the disturbing evidence of a traitor in the military camp bringing reinforcements. When they arrived at the military camp to find them all missing, Kyle simply activated the embedded trackers under their skin. And the rest as they say was history.

Life went on. Those in Kodiak Point resumed their lives—and their furry pastimes.

There was much rejoicing by the time the winter solstice rolled around.

Not only had they vanquished their enemy, but the town had also grown in the last year. Grown stronger both in numbers and determination as a clan.

Their leader, Reid, and his wife, Tammy, had seen them through some tough times. The alpha of Kodiak point had shown himself capable and fearless. He'd also helped father a new generation. Twins actually, a boy and girl, and while Dr. Jess claimed they were bears, even she couldn't tell with certainty yet which parent they would take after. But there was no denying both children bore alpha traits. Their lusty yells, rapid growth, and keen intelligence shone through. Or so the proud papa claimed, and who was going to argue the point with a Kodiak bear?

Boris as a berserker with a gun in hand was scary. As a moose, who trampled anything in his path and, despite his blunt rack, managed to ram a man and shove until his innards squished, he was impressive. Now imagine Boris, paired with his father-in-law, determined to protect a sassy blonde vixen who was almost seven months pregnant with his daughter. Fucking terrifying.

"Move out of the way. Precious coming through," Boris could be heard blaring when Jan went grocery shopping.

Or...

"Boris, put me down. I am perfectly capable of walking up steps," from his exasperated mate, Jan, who might protest aloud but wore a smug smile at the adoration Boris showed her. An adoration that turned into fierce, bloodthirsty pride when her mate pounded the hell out of Munroe when he dared buy the last carton of pecan caramel ice cream.

His excuse, as Boris cradled the dented box under his arm and glared at the moaning heap? "Jan's craving."

Then there was Gene and Vicky. Sweet girl that Vicky. Kind. Soft spoken. Cute if you liked the geeky type. And completely oblivious when it came to Gene. She thought him a hero.

Snort.

But she was allowed her delusions; she was human. That and Gene threatened to kill anyone who told her otherwise.

Then there was Kyle. Manwhore Kyle, who settled into domestication with Crystal and her daughter, Gigi, like a duck to orange glaze sauce. Once upon a time, he might have roamed the wild, but now, only one pair of panties adorned his mighty rack. He also was a scary glimpse into how scarred ex-soldiers were as dads. He worshipped the little girl he adopted. Make her cry and you'd better run. Daddy Kyle didn't let no one mess with his little girl.

It seemed no one was immune to the love bug. Even Brody, the man who craved adventure fell victim and, of course, found a lady to suit his needs. Layla might have spent years as a prisoner seeing nothing of the world, but she'd done her best to rectify that since she and Brody had escaped. With Reid's blessing, they were off traipsing Europe at the moment. Getting thrown into jails for spying, allegedly. Not that they let something like incarceration ruin their fun. Or so the postcards claimed. Springing themselves and leading the authorities on a merry chase was their idea of a good time. A perfect life for a man and a woman who weren't ready for a white-picket-fence-type of life.

And what about Travis and Jess, you might ask. Well, once Betty-Sue got over the shock of Travis moving out—no amount of pie in the world could drag that boy back from the much sweeter dessert found between his wife's thighs—they came to a truce, especially once Betty-Sue realized she was going to be a grandma.

Poor Jess. It would be a miracle if she ended up able to walk with all the food Betty-Sue was determined to make her eat.

As for me. Who am I you might wonder that I know so much about the town and its inhabitants? I was the town recluse, living there quietly and healing from the war. Left alone because that's what I wanted. What I needed.

But now?

Now I think it's time for me to maybe go back home where I belong. The swamp is calling me.

The past is no longer haunting me. Much.

It's time this crocodile stopped hibernating and faced the world.

And took a bite out of life.

The End

For more Eve Langlais stories please visit www.EveLanglais.com

CPSIA information can be obtained
at www.ICGtesting.com
Printed in the USA
LVOW04s1709300516
490484LV00060B/1977/P